The Ghosts of Kennesaw Mountain

By

Lois Helmers
&
Gerald Harding Gunn

Badgley Publishing Company
Canal Winchester, Ohio

2011

ISBN-13: 978-0-9854403-0-5

ISBN-10: 0985440309

2nd Edition April 6, 2012

Contents

Chapter 1

I awoke to a dreary, cold day on February 21, 2011 in Atlanta, Georgia. Well, it was cold for Georgia, a brisk 20 degrees. It had been a cold winter this year, but I was born and raised in Columbus, Ohio and should be able to handle such a mild temperature. I had walked to school after all, in blizzards and minus 0 temperatures not too many years before. Looking out the bedroom window gave me a chill and made me roll over, pull up the covers, and wish I did not have to get up.

I came here with the expectation that Atlanta was warmer. True, there was rarely snow, it did not dip down to zero very often, but 20 degrees seemed colder than Columbus with its snow and chill. Atlanta is supposed to be warmer, warmer than back home. Well, at least there's no snow on the ground, and I don't have to worry about getting up and going out in it and walking to school, but I do have to go to work. Wednesday, damn, it's only Wednesday, Wednesday and 20 degrees, I really don't want to go to work!

Janet and Jane, the 'early birds', are already gone, but I hear Barbara rustling around. She's making coffee, bless her little heart, and I'm going to need that blessed black hot drink to get me going. "Hey, lady of leisure," I heard her call out, without seeing her, but knew she was dressed and ready to go in her smart blue stewardess uniform with red trim. "Unless you won the lottery in your sleep, have become a millionaire, and can stay in bed and do what you want to, you better get your fanny out of bed! Come on, get up and have a cup of coffee with me before I have to hit the door and go. Got a flight to 'Frisco' this morning, but have no fear, I'll be back by Friday evening, ready to get you and the other two in some kind of mischief."

As I put on my robe I still could not see her face but I knew there was an impish smirk on it. As I entered the kitchen, Barbara poured a cup of coffee and handed it to me. "Well, you look fit to kill.

Not sure I like that saying just before a flight" Barbara replied with a grin. "Why don't you just say, thanks for making the coffee and handing me a cup, and I hope you have a safe trip, but I'm glad you're impressed with my appearance."

I grinned back as I took a sip of the warm liquid and let it start to wake me up. "O.K., thanks for the coffee and I hope you have a safe trip, and who knows, I might have a surprise for you when you get back."

Off she goes, I thought, as I watched her in her overcoat, buffeting herself against the cold as she unlocked her car to get ready to drive to the airport. You should have cranked up the car, let it warm up, and come back inside for a little while instead of just going out and just jumping in the damn thing and letting yourself in for a chilly ride to the airport, gal, I thought.

But when Barbara is in a hurry and thinks she's running behind, she only has one gear and that's 'fast forward.' Her old 2001 Toyota Camry grudgingly came to life after she hopped in, and in a minute she was down the driveway and gone. Barbara is only a few inches taller than me, with reddish-brown hair and green eyes. She wanted to travel, see the world, used to tell me so over and over when we were in school back in Columbus. "I want adventure, want to explore, I want to get out of Columbus!", and she did.

She was the first of our foursome to land a job after she graduated, right here in Atlanta.

I could count on Barbara, maybe more than Janet and Jane to understand; we share the same wanderlust, the same sense of inquiry about the past; we are all loyal to each other, caring, protective, but Barbara is the loyal friend who knows my longing for what was in the world, in my family, long before I was here, long before any of us were here.

It's got to be more than just coincidence that the four of us, Janet, Jane, Barbara and I all came to Georgia, to Atlanta, just out of college, to find jobs, buy a house and start a life here, but I still have trouble believing it...Why Georgia, why Atlanta, I continue to ask myself. Not complaining you understand. We're all having a heck of a good time as foot loose, fancy free females looking for good days and good times. And was it pure luck alone that we all landed the jobs we were hoping and longing for, jobs that fitted our desires, talents and personalities?

And this three story house in Buckhead, the perfect place, the perfect location, for the 'Four Musketeers', it all seems to fit together so well, so why are you still not happy with your life, girl? What keeps pulling you, tugging you, to be someone else, somewhere else?

It was still hard for me to believe that we have been in Georgia for two years. We came here as new college graduates.

Barbara Warren, Janet Evans, Jane O'Keefe and me, Kathleen Kelley, were the 'Four Musketeers', a name we laughingly adopted when we were sophomores at Central High School. We were inseparable, stuck like glue together always. All had our separate interests, but we were together more than we were apart. When we were seniors, we all decided we couldn't be parted, so we all went to college at Ohio State. Barbara majored in Psychology, Janet and Jane in Finance, and I opted for History. It was the only class in high school I really seemed to excel in, and it always held my interest.

Barbara, the flight attendant, in fine position, by the way, to land herself a good looking, well paid man. Janet Evans and Jane O'Keefe, both math whizzes, the financial analysts, secure and satisfied with their jobs and me Kathleen Kelley, the executive assistant who incredibly has a prince for a boss, and a good looking, single prince at that.

Barbara chose her vocation wisely because she loves to travel and see new sights. She is the most adventurous of our group; you will always find her exploring on her own, away from the rest of us. Barbara is the loyal friend everyone wishes they had. You can always count on her to take care of the details while at the same time making you feel like a million dollars.

Janet is the tallest of us, with beautiful rich brown hair, bold brown eyes, and the sunniest disposition of anyone I have ever met. She's a hard worker and totally loyal to her company – she's the kind who never works just 40 hours a week, she always gives those extra few hours, but she always has time for her friends. I can't tell you how many times she's been there for me to either cry on her shoulder or laugh at the crazy things we do together. She is definitely the take-charge person of our group. She is also a 'techie', the smartest person I know when it comes to a computer or any software program.

Jane is much like Janet, but has a more devil-may-care attitude. She is always the first to get us in trouble, but she is always the first to come to our rescue too. She is just a little shorter than Janet, with brown hair and green eyes, and is the most fun-loving of the group; always the person most likely to be the life of the party and the most popular of us all. She is also a softie and very sentimental, although she would never admit it. When watching a sad movie, Jane is always the first to cry. She is also the first to help a stranger or buy the last box of Girl Scout cookies because the girl needs to sell it to win a prize.

Janet and Jane are both Financial Analysts with JYM Transportation Company and love their jobs. Barbara is a flight attendant with Smiling Airways and is happy as a lark. And I have my dream job as the Executive Assistant to the CEO of Smart Enterprises,

Inc. My job is challenging, my boss is understanding and easy to work with; I make a great income, and I'm just not completely happy. I must have been born with wanderlust in my veins because there always seems to be something calling to me that I never quite seem to find.

I was the only child of Douglas and Lena Kelley and grew up in Columbus, Ohio. Dad was a machinist at a small machine shop at Port Columbus Airport and Mom was a housewife.

Growing up as an only child in a mid-sized town in the Midwest, proved extremely boring for me. I had few friends when I was in elementary school, I was too bossy and too much a loner to attract friends for long. The few bright moments in my childhood occurred on visits to my parent's home town of Chester, Ohio. Every summer from the time I was five until I was 16 we would make the drive from Columbus to Chester, about an hour and a half drive. We stayed with friends of my Dad, the Callihans. There was Glenn and Sis and their children, Charlie, Glenn Junior and Mary Margaret. My Dad and Glenn loved to play the guitar and I loved to listen. Their music ranged from Gospel to Rock and Roll, and many nights they sat on the front porch after dinner and played until the early morning.

Charlie, Glenn Junior and Mary Margaret were my first real friends. They taught me where to find tadpoles, how to fish and how to pick blackberries. They tried to teach me how to milk a cow, but this city girl could just not figure it out, and they gave up trying. It was there in Chester where I had my first crush on a red-haired boy by the name of Brad at the tender age of thirteen. It didn't last long that crush, but it was a memorable time of my life. These people taught me to share, to care for others and taught me the true meaning of friendship.

During my junior year in high school my Dad died of a heart attack while at work, I'll never forget that terrible phone call after, but the days following will always remain a blur. Without my friends I don't think I could have faced that next year. They got me through heartbreak, sadness, anger...all those feelings one experiences after a great loss. They left me alone when I wanted only to grieve. They made me get out and get on with life, even though all I wanted to do was hideaway and be left alone. I will love these friends forever if for no other reason than for being there for me when I needed them the most.

After graduation, Barbara was the first to land a job in Atlanta, Georgia. We all discussed at length our job opportunities in Ohio, but where one goes...we must all follow, so we put out our resumes to the best companies in Atlanta. I was next to receive a letter requesting my presence for an interview. On July 7th I flew to Atlanta, met with the Human Resource Director of Smart Enterprises and the CEO, Brad Huntington. Impressed was definitely the word I thought of after the interview. Benefits were fantastic, Brad seemed very nice and I could see myself enjoying keeping him organized and on time for every meeting.

After the interview, I met with Janie Bryson, real estate agent for Century Real Estate, and drove around the area to look at housing, just as a lark, I thought. Janie suggested that Buckhead would be an ideal place for me since it was close to Smart Enterprises and not too far from the airport for Barbara's airline job.

The first house she showed me I fell in love with...a very large four bedroom, five bath house on a large, 1½ acre lot. The first things that caught my eye were the many windows, and the three stories with radiant sunshine overhead! I think there is less sunshine in Ohio than pretty much anywhere I know of. There were cardinals and blue jays cavorting among the many hardwood trees in the yard, singing a welcoming greeting, it seemed to me at that moment.

I toured the house, thinking to myself this was the perfect house for me, the house I wanted to live in for quite awhile. All the bedrooms were large; the master had a fireplace and a sitting room. The closet was huge, a perfectly organized 9' square that any female would love to have.

The kitchen was large with an island in the middle, great for entertaining and cooking for a crowd, I counted twelve cabinets, all white as snow and sighed with longing, thinking of the many meals I would enjoy cooking in this beautiful room. There was a nice screened-in porch just off the kitchen for summer enjoyment. A small creek ran along the back of the property giving the wonderful sound of a bubbling brook. The exterior of the house was a light colored brick; perfect low maintenance for us females. Of course, I didn't tell Janie I loved it, just said it was very nice and I would get back with her. I had only time to look at one more home, and was not impressed at all with the layout of that one. I knew that first house was the one I wanted to spend time in, a place to call home and to make memories in.

I researched Buckhead on the flight back to Ohio and found that Buckhead was known as Irbyville for Henry Irby, who purchased 203 acres in 1838 for $650.00. The area was occupied by the Cherokee and Creek Indians prior to Mr. Irby's purchase. I could just imagine Indians in back of the house roasting venison and children scampering in the creek.

My friends mean the world to me, I can always count on them and they bring me the most joy in my life. Whether together, or going our separate ways, I know they will always be there for me. I love being in Atlanta with my best friends but still, something is missing for me...I just don't know what it is.

Maybe it's because I'm 5' 0" tall, have bright green eyes, weigh 100 pounds and have bright red hair. Maybe it comes from my Irish and Scottish ancestors who moved from Ireland and Scotland to Meigs County, Ohio in 1858 to work in the glass houses and coal mines. Something or someone is calling to me to find something; I just have to keep looking.

Well, I've procrastinated long enough, time to get in the shower and get dressed for the day. I have a 2 hour meeting today and probably an hour drive to work. My office is only 12 miles from the house, but sometimes in Atlanta traffic it takes me an hour to get there. Think I'll wear my red power suit today, along with my three inch heels and impress the heck out of em all!

Chapter 2

It is finally Friday and I'm almost home. Coming home to a house I love is a balm to my soul after five days and 50 hours at work. The house we bought was the first one I looked at on my job interview trip to Georgia. Jane loves the fact that we have 1 ½ acres...she loves to mow the lawn and take care of the outside, while the rest of us don't care for yard work so we take her indoor chores. She even named her lawn mower Murray and takes better care of it than I do my car. She religiously takes it for a tune-up each year, washes it weekly and waxes it once a year.

"I'm home," I say as I unlock the front door. "Where's the wine?"

Barbara answered "You know we have a glass ready for you. Sunny California was just that, but I'm glad I'm home! How was your day?"

Janet and Jane chimed in at the same time "Hi, TGIF girlfriend, happy Friday and happy weekend."

"Hi guys," I say, "TGIF to all of you. I had a good, very long week and would like to unwind this weekend. How about a nice visit to Kennesaw Mountain! You know we've been here for two years now and I have not visited a single history site...I must be losing my mind...would you please, please all go with me tomorrow?"

Everyone laughingly said "OK, OK we can't believe it's taken you this long."

"I know it's cold today, but it's supposed to get to 48 degrees tomorrow, we can bundle up and most of our time will be spent in the museum anyway, so it will be warm there."

I have been researching my family history recently and just discovered that three of my Kelley ancestors served in the Civil War. They were in the 63rd Ohio Volunteer Infantry. Guess where they fought...right here in Atlanta, GA, small world huh? Benjamin Kelley enlisted at the age of 23 and was a Corporal. His brother Lewis enlisted when he was 17 and Henry at the very young age of 15, both were privates. I wanted to see exactly where the 63rd had fought at Kennesaw Mountain, and I wanted the girls to go with me to find out. My ancestors were all listed as being at Kennesaw Mountain, and I couldn't wait to visit the area, it has taken me two years to have time to think about my love of history and there was so much available within a two hour drive of my home.

"OK guys," I said, "Let's leave about 11:00 a.m. so we can visit the museum and then drive to the battle site."

Janet said "You really owe me for this you know, I really don't care that much for history but will do it for you...but, since you're dragging me to a boring museum, you can go with me next week to the Atlanta History Center. You've gotten me interested in researching my family – I guess I can start there."

Jane chimed in, "You know I really don't care about dead people or history, but I'll go with you because you're a friend, but you can go with me to a party on Tuesday, I heard there were some really cool people going to be there and I don't want to go alone."

"All right Jane, I'll go with you if you'll go with me."

We all prepared a culinary feast of veggies, cheese and a salad, a feast for single girls in the 21st Century. We were all watching our weight, as usual, and in addition to the wine we were indulging in, that's about all the calories we were willing to count. After dinner, Barbara washed the dishes, I dried and Janet swept the kitchen floor.

Jane said "While you girls are cleaning up the kitchen, I'm going to cue in a movie. When you're done, you want to join me?"

"Yes, said Janet."

"Count me in" said Barbara.

"Me too, I said, but I don't want to stay up real late... I want to save myself for tomorrow! I guess you all expect me to drive, but I was already planning on that. Don't let me forget the camera. I definitely want lots of pictures. Who knows, maybe I'll take a picture of a ghost, I've heard many people have seen them there."

Jane had that smirk on her face that appeared every time I came up with something she thought was wacky. "Picture of a ghost?" she quipped. "How do you take a picture of a ghost, I thought they were transparent. Hell, Kath, I'll bet if you saw a spook out there you'd drop your little digital and run for your life, HA HA HA. Besides we're going out there during the day, I thought ghosts haunted at night. I don't believe in ghosts, the unexplained is a fact, I'll admit, but I don't know about those ghosts."

"I don't know either, smarty," I replied. "I do know that ghosts are known to haunt because issues in a person's life went unresolved before they died suddenly for some reason, and a lot of people die suddenly in a battle. As for a ghost at Kennesaw Mountain, we'll just have to see, won't we?"

Chapter 3

By 10:00 a.m. Saturday morning the threat of rain appeared over, it was beginning to warm up to the promised mid forties and so far at least the girls were not beginning to back out going with me.

Barbara glanced out the window and yawned. "You know Kath, if you weren't such a close friend since my childhood, I'd be damned if I would be giving up my Saturday morning, when I prefer to lay around and be lazy, and go with you to this battlefield that you are so fascinated with."

"Same here!" Janet and Jane echoed, both rubbing their eyes while they drank their morning coffee. "You are going to buy us lunch, right?" Janet replied.

"Yes, of course" I said. "And you're in for a treat...skip the diet food for the day gals, we'll dine at Cracker Barrel."

That announcement seemed to cheer everybody up as I urged my little band of reluctant historians to finish getting dressed and began herding them to the car, which I had already warmed up. Refreshingly, there was very little traffic on I-75 north to Marietta or on Barrett Parkway. We traveled through an area that was once farm and woodland at the time of the battle but was now a place crammed with strip shopping centers, gas stations and restaurants. "Oh, there's the Cracker Barrel, yum, yum! don't forget your promise," Janet chimed in as we moved closer to the left turn where park signs pointed to the battlefield.

"I won't...don't worry," I said, watching for the turn that would take us back to the time of roaring cannon, crackling musket fire, and struggling soldiers. Old U.S. 41 took us through bare hardwood trees, the sun shining through bare limbs not yet kissed by the promise of spring. The woods looked rather gaunt...kind of haunting. Here the urban encroachment stopped and the further we traveled toward the battlefield, the more it seemed that we were seeing what land looked like in 1864, when my ancestors in Federal blue were drawn here to fight the Rebels in gray and butternut. We moved up the old two-lane highway, and then we saw it, the twin peaks of Kennesaw Mountain, with the Cherokee name that no one had a clear idea of the meaning.

The park entrance guided us to the visitor center; Big Kennesaw rose behind it, nearly 800 feet above us, and to the southwest was Little Kennesaw, Pigeon Hill, named for the now extinct birds that once roosted there, and from there, Cheatham Hill, where the main attack occurred that hot, bloody late June day so long ago. It was Sherman's last mountain, the last mountain in his way and he had to drive the Confederates from it before he could move on to Atlanta.

"Well, glad we're here, I'm ready to stretch," Jane remarked as she got out of the car. "Bet it is really pretty up here in the spring, kind of plain looking right now with no leaves on the trees though."

I couldn't help but notice the many people walking dogs and lots of joggers and thought to myself that it was kind of a sacrilege at a place where so many men and boys had died in battle.

As we walked up to the visitor center and museum entrance, a field artillery piece mounted for display near the door briefly caught Janet's attention. It was one of those long-barreled cannon with a band around the breach. Janet read the plaque identifying it.

"A Parrott gun", she read out loud, and then a smirk formed on her lips. "Why on earth would they have such a big gun just to shoot at parrots, they're such harmless and colorful little birds."

I knew she was just playing dumb and at the same time trying to rattle my chain. "I don't think they used it to shoot at parrots Janet," I replied dryly. "I think that's the name of the man who invented the cannon. Clearly you're in need of a Civil War education...now get in here before you make any more silly remarks."

We entered the front door of the museum and were greeted by a park ranger who introduced himself as 'Willie'. "Morning ladies", he said, "how can I help you today?"

I chimed up immediately "I'm interested in learning more about the 63rd Ohio Volunteer Infantry. I understand they were here during the battle."

Willie answered "Well, let's take a look at our records and find out where they were, follow me."

We all followed and he went into an office and came out a little later with a very large book. He thumbed through a few pages and said "Here they are, afraid they weren't in the battle, they were held in reserve in an area that is now a very upscale subdivision. It's called, oddly enough, 'The Reserve'. You exit out of the park here, turn left, it's about 2 miles on your left." Willie continued, "There were a lot of troops from Ohio here though during the battle and included the following volunteer infantry units: 5th, 15th, 19th, 26th, 27th, 32nd, 40th, 46th, 47th, 51st, 52nd, 53rd, 57th, 61st, 64th, 65th, 74th, 78th, 90th, 93rd, 97th, 98th, 99th, 101st, 113th, 121st and the 125th OVI – that's a lot of Ohio boys."

As Willie was mentioning all those Ohio soldiers, I recalled reading about an Oscar Jackson from the 63rd Ohio Volunteer Infantry, Company C, and his tales about fighting here, perhaps the records weren't totally correct, maybe a few of the 63rd were here in action. I can't tell you how disappointed I was though, I had this feeling that my ancestors were here and I was somehow following in their footsteps! "Oh well" I said, "I still would like to take a look at the area after our visit here."

Willie said "You all should see the film we have on the battle. It depicts quite accurately the battle and is only fifteen minutes long. Please look around the museum, there's lots to see, and if there is anything else I can help you with, please let me know."

Janet took me off to the side and whispered "I'm so sorry Kath, I know you wanted to learn more about your ancestors who were here, and maybe we'll find something else later. Let's go see the film and learn more about what happened here."

We all followed the signs to the auditorium where the film was scheduled to be shown in five minutes.

We took our seats and waited with about thirty others to watch the film.

The film began with Sherman's Federal forces advancing on June 10, 1864 to Marietta to protect his supply line. They were hampered by weeks of rain, then on June 19th Sherman's troops forced Johnston to withdraw, but he withdrew to a prepared position at Kennesaw Mountain, a large humped ridge with rocky slopes. Confederate engineers had created a line of entrenchments covering every approaching ravine with cannon and rifle. Sherman advanced south to get around the Confederates, but Johnston countered by sending 11,000 men under General John Bell Hood to meet the threat. At Kolb's Farm on June 22nd, Hood tried unsuccessfully to defeat Sherman. On June 27th at 8:00a.m., the Battle of Kennesaw began in earnest. Union brigades with 5,500 men approached Pigeon Hill, but the Confederate line held by rolling large rocks downhill at the Federal forces. At the same time, another force of 8,000 Union infantry attacked Johnston's army commanded by Generals Patrick R. Cleburne and Benjamin Franklin Cheatham. Many of those in this attack were shot down, and there was a brutal hand-to-hand combat on top of the defenders' earthworks. Both sides named this place the "Dead Angle." The North lost 3,000 men, the Confederates lost 1,000. By July 2nd the area was abandoned by both sides. By the end of the film I had cold chills running up and down my arms and I knew I had to see this Cheatham Hill.

After the film we toured the museum. To our right and left was an exhibit of the army commanders for the Union and the Confederacy, the commanders of the Atlanta Campaign...we saw the rebel regimental flags and original soldier uniforms, then the weapons the men used, along with their equipment...an exhibit on how the armies deployed and fought...the room featured the very cannon in the Confederate works guarding Atlanta that was photographed by George Barnard, the wet plate photographer who traveled with Sherman's armies.

After the museum I picked up a brochure that showed a self-guided auto tour. "Are you ladies up for just a couple more stops? I want to drive over to Cheatham Hill next and then stop by to see 'The Reserve', and then it's on to lunch at the Cracker Barrel." Everyone agreed on the stops and we made our way to my car.

"You know, it was a terrible time, back then, wasn't it," Jane remarked as we headed toward Cheatham Hill. "I mean, all those young men and boys, fighting and shooting at each other and killing each other that day, and this was happening for four years. And they, most of them, had the same background, spoke the same language, worshiped the same God. They were so alike, yet so different too."

"Sounds like our visit is provoking some thought" I said, smiling as we approached the turn off to the part of the battlefield where the worst fighting and casualties had occurred. "Are you at least a little glad you came along today?" I asked.

"Yeah, yeah I think I am," Jane replied. "You know, I never thought about it much, frankly, until today. History to me was just studying a text book so I could pass the test and then move on, and the books never told me what really happened. I felt I just had to memorize names of places, names of people, and then dump it into test answers to get a passing grade."

Our museum visit had given me the same incentive to pause and think and imagine, but with a difference. Unlike Jane, I had distant blood relations who were here who experienced the horror, probably saw or knew that fellow Ohio farm boys were dying or were maimed that day.

"Well, I have studied and learned a bit more about that war" Janet said. "I've read about Gettysburg, Antietam, and Shiloh and what happened there. You know as I recall, they really did not know what they were getting into until it was too late. At the beginning they all thought it was going to amount to just a three or six month fracas and then it would be over. It turned out it was the worst man-made disaster in our history, maybe in any nation's history."

Barbara, I noticed, was silent and I saw a reflective, faraway expression on her face when I glanced at her in the rear view mirror. As I would learn later, she, like me, was being taken back in time, was trying to peer through the many decades to that day of destiny for so many Americans, North and South, to that day of blood and thick, sulphery gun smoke and death.

Chapter 4

We were the only car on the road to Cheatham Hill. It was eerily quiet; it was still a gray cool day and I guess there weren't many people out and about because of the weather.

We slowed and then stopped to read a plaque on our right. The sign described a terrible fire that broke out in the woods, threatening the men of the North of being burned alive. A cease-fire was issued and both the North and South worked to drag the helpless Union men to safety.

I pulled back onto the road, driving slowly – we were all quiet, thinking what an awful day that had been so many years before. Jane was the first to speak, saying "I thought this was going to be an enjoyable day, not this sad, awful reminder of a war almost 150 years ago."

"That's why we come to historical sites – we need to recall what tremendous sacrifices our ancestors gave for our freedom" I said.

"We're almost to the area where the worst fighting took place, Cheatham Hill. Guess we don't have to worry about finding a parking place, no one else is here."

We parked and walked the short distance to the area known as the 'Dead Angle.' "You can still see the earthworks" Kathleen said, as we came upon the area where the Confederates had dug in and were waiting on the Union soldiers.

Next we wandered over to the Illinois monument. My tour brochure said, and I read to the group, that it was dedicated to the Union survivors exactly fifty years after the battle. It also said that McCook's brigade lost 397 men at Cheatham Hill in a half hour.

I also described the area, showing them where the Union soldiers had come from, just over a crest to meet the waiting Confederates. As we were all looking at the crest, I saw four Union soldiers, holding guns, who seemed to move very quickly and then disappear. I blinked my eyes several times and shook my head and wondered if I had just imagined the image... after all, we were looking at an area where many soldiers had been.

I looked at the others and saw Jane shaking her head and blinking her eyes. "Jane, did you see something on that crest? Did you Barbara and Janet?"

Jane said "I'm not sure, it happened so fast, but I think I saw soldiers!"

Janet and Barbara looked at us in disbelief and said "I didn't see anything. You guys are just making that up to scare us."

"I swear I saw Union soldiers and they were holding large guns" I said. Jane and I both started crying. A terribly sad feeling had overcome us and all we could do was stand there and cry.

Jane said "I don't believe what I just saw, but I know I saw it. Don't you ever bring me here again, or anywhere else where there might be a ghost, I don't like it and I don't want to believe it, but there it was. No one is ever going to believe me anyway; Hell, I don't even want to tell anyone."

Janet and Barbara just looked at us and Barbara said "Do you swear you're telling us the truth? We were right there with you and we didn't see anything." Then she said, "I think they're telling the truth because they're both white in the face and Kath is sweating like a pig in 40 degree weather, something must have happened. Let's just keep this to ourselves and not talk about it anymore today. We're going to have to check if there have been any other sightings of ghosts in this area and do some more research...we can do that at the Atlanta History Center this week Kath."

I dried my eyes and agreed with Janet, I didn't want to think about this anymore today either. "OK, guys, let's get out of here and go have lunch."

We all walked back to my car, no one said a word as we drove out of the park. I just can't believe what happened today, but I sure want to learn a lot more about this area and what caused Jane and me to see the same thing.

Lunch was a pretty quiet affair; we talked about trivial things, about how good lunch was, that we hoped Spring would be here soon, that we needed to get our taxes taken care of, and that we were all a little tired and ready to head home.

The drive home was uneventful and everyone headed in opposite directions when we reached the front door. We all had a lot to think about... our trip to Kennesaw Mountain.

Chapter 5

I immediately went to my bedroom and turned on my laptop. While I was waiting for it to boot up I walked to the kitchen and poured myself a glass of wine; I definitely needed this after the day I had just experienced.

I walked back to my bedroom and sat down at my computer. I Googled "ghosts at Kennesaw Mountain" and was amazed that 30 hits came up. I clicked on the first hit and saw a web site that was dedicated to ghost sightings at various civil war sites. I clicked on the link to Kennesaw Mountain.

A site appeared that showed a man called 'Pappy' who had been to Kennesaw Mountain on March 28th, 2001. He had visited the exact area of Cheatham Hill that we had been to today. He reported that he had seen four Union soldiers dressed in blue, carrying Enfield Rifles. They wore the Federal campaign cap, based on the French Kepi on their heads, and all were young, very young – in his estimation probably 18 to 20 years old. He recalled they appeared to be on guard duty, and they appeared to him for only about 2 seconds and then they vanished.

Pappy turned out to be Professor Charles Wilcox, professor of American History at Kennesaw State University. He said he was working on a research paper. He listed his phone number and asked that if anyone had experienced a similar sighting that they contact him. I was totally in shock as I thought that he experienced the exact same thing that Jane and I had experienced today. This validated something that I thought perhaps I had imagined. I was totally psyched; my heartbeat had accelerated, my palms were sweaty and I had to sit back in my chair and contemplate what this really meant.

I yelled out at the top of my lungs, "Girls, you have got to come and see what I just found!"

Jane ran in to my room first, "What did you find? I told you I don't want to talk about what happened today. I don't want to know anything about what you found, I really don't. I don't think I can stand to even think about it ever again!"

I could tell she meant what she said, and I was truly sorry that it had upset her so much. Barbara showed up next, saying "I thought we weren't going to talk about this anymore today, but I am curious."

Janet showed up next, "OK, what did you find?"

I proceeded to tell them about Professor Wilcox and his sightings.

Janet said "Well, if this Professor saw exactly what you say you and Jane saw, I guess there must be something there, some energy field or something we don't even understand. We need to contact someone who knows a whole lot more about this subject than we do, and we know next to nothing. You are going to have to do a lot more research on the subject of paranormal happenings, and more importantly specifically in this area. I don't know about the rest of you, but I've had enough for one day...I totally believe you, because I know you and you wouldn't fabricate something this important to you. I know that history is very close to your heart, but I think this is even beyond your love of history. I have a feeling, and I could be totally wrong, but I have a very strange feeling that this is very specific to you."

"OK, I just wanted to share what I found and to let you know that it's not just our imaginations. I feel like you Janet, that I'm supposed to look into this, and I think you're right, I too have this feeling that these ghosts or apparitions or whatever you want to call them were saying something to me in particular. I'll keep you all informed, but I won't involve any of you, unless of course you want to be involved. Let's get some rest tonight and maybe some clue will come to me in my dreams. Goodnight all!"

Chapter 6

I slept fitfully that night, but nothing came to me in my dreams to help me understand those strange happenings yesterday. I still had that strange feeling that something else was going to happen, something important to my future.

As usual, Janet was already up and brewing coffee when I meandered into the kitchen. "Good morning" she said. "Any dreams of ghosts?"

"No" I said, "but I didn't sleep very well, couldn't seem to get comfortable or maybe my mind was just working overtime in my sleep. Sure looking forward to that coffee. I'm going out to get the newspaper."

I opened the front door and smiled on hearing the many birds in the trees in the yard; I never got tired of listening to the music they made in the morning. I retrieved the paper, shut the door and headed to the kitchen for that first cup of coffee.

I poured my coffee and sat down at the table, opened the newspaper and was astounded to see Professor Wilcox on the front page; it was an article about his publication of a paper on ghosts at Kennesaw Mountain. This was just too much to see on a Sunday morning after seeing ghosts yesterday. Was something or someone telling me something? I knew then that I had to talk to Professor Wilcox as soon as possible.

I showed the paper to Janet who read the article. She raised her eyebrows, cocked her head and said "Looks like talking to Professor Wilcox about ghosts is

on your agenda in the not too distant future
girlfriend."

Chapter 7

Charles Wilcox put the copy of the Journal on the kitchen counter and poured his first cup of Sunday morning coffee before he unfolded the overly thick weekend edition, full of the usual weekend ads and circulars full of bright colored pictures of merchandise he did not want to own, and did not have the money to buy even if he did.

"First things first," he said out loud to himself. It was alright to speak out loud to no one but himself, but he would have been speaking to Mamie, if she was still alive and still sharing their modest garden flat together in West Atlanta, where they had lived for two years since the foreclosure took their three bedroom home on the North side of town that had been their home for 30 years.

Mamie had taken ill four years ago, diagnosed with cancer. They had spent all their life savings trying to beat that cancer; trying to be together for just a little while longer.

When he opened the paper he saw his image staring back at him, the headline reading: *"History Prof knows the Ghosts of Kennesaw."*

"Ha!" he exclaimed "Ha, Ha, they published it, must be having a slow Sunday. Wonder why they put it on the front page and not the feature section?"

He had to admit the piece attracted his attention, and for the moment took his mind off the loneliness that had plagued him since the death of his wife, three months ago.

He still spoke to her as if she was there; she would have said, "Well, Charlie, go ahead and read it to me, I know you're just dying to," and her sky blue eyes would have twinkled and laughed and she would have smiled at him.

"Well darlin', looks like your bald-headed old man made the front page," he said to the woman who was no longer there, and who he missed so much that it was an effort to just get up in the morning.

He was pleased the reporter, her name was Erin Jenkins, had quoted him correctly and wrote in a style and with prose that did not make him look like some aged, peculiar eccentric.

He had told her of that day, that day when he saw the four shadowy Federals appear not 20 yards in front of him at the Cheatham Hill trenches, right at the Bloody Angle where those Illinois farm boys tried to breach General Joseph Johnston's line and ran head on into farm boys from Tennessee, that sultry mid morning so many generations ago. But to him, time had evaporated that morning; that morning he saw them and he knew he was looking at men as they appeared that day. He knew what they looked like from his years of studying what happened and from his years of actually portraying them and their Rebel enemies in the numerous living history events and re-enactments, too many to recall. He had spoken to others who had witnessed those Federals also, and had researched in depth what had happened that day at Kennesaw Mountain.

During those years he had picked up the nickname 'Pappy'. He really did not know why except that he was older than most of the men and boys in the 'hobby' and was much more knowledgeable about the soldiers of both sides than most of them. They had learned from him, learned how to improve their impressions and look more like the men they were portraying. They had learned from him in the classroom at Kennesaw University as well. Many students credited him with 'putting flesh on the bones of history', and making it real and relevant to them.

He became so well known as 'Pappy' Wilcox that many people did not know him by his real name. Of course, Mamie kept calling him Charlie, even when she joined him in period dress and camped with him at the events. She had picked up a nickname also, that of 'Mrs. Pappy' and she was a popular and familiar fixture around camp, especially when she cooked for everyone, and she was one hell of a camp cook. Her specialty was mouth-watering homemade biscuits that no one could refuse.

They had visited most of the major battle sites together; Resaca, Tunnel Hill, Gettysburg, Antietam, Winchester, Bull Run, The Wilderness, Bentonville, North Carolina, Chickamauga, and had even gone to Andersonville where so many prisoners died. They were hoping to go to Shiloh and Corinth but that was when Mamie had taken sick and they had not been able to go. So many memories, all good ones!

So the article was good, he thought, nothing out of context, and he hoped it might spark or rekindle interest in history and what happened that day at Cheatham Hill. Of course, he also hoped he would not get the reputation as a 'ghost hunter'. He would leave that to those guys on the 'Sci-Fi' channel on cable TV.

The memory of Mamie in her brown print dress, white apron and bonnet stirring a cook pot over the fire had made him smile; he was holding the memory close to him in his mind when the phone rang.

"Is this Professor Wilcox, Pappy Wilcox?" a breathless female voice asked.

"Yes," he replied. "Who is this?"

"My name is Kathleen Kelley, Professor Wilcox," the voice replied. "I saw the ghosts that you mentioned on your website and in today's newspaper article. I saw them just yesterday, and I'm confused, slightly afraid and a little bewildered at seeing them appear out of nowhere. I was hoping to meet you and discuss them a little more if that would be OK with you."

Chapter 8

"Whoa young lady, hold up there just a minute," Pappy said. "Are you telling me that you saw exactly what I described on my web page and in today's newspaper?"

"Yes sir" I said, and I am just so excited I just can hardly stand it. My girlfriends sort of think I'm crazy, but another friend saw the same thing at the same time that I did, so I think that makes it more than just coincidence, don't you, but I sound like I'm rambling and I guess I am."

"So now you're saying that two of you saw the ghosts at the same time?" Pappy asked.

"Yes sir, like I said I'm just so excited I can't speak and make myself understood right now. Would it be OK to meet so we can talk more about this" I asked.

"I would love to meet you Kathleen" Pappy said, "how about next Saturday at Kennesaw Mountain, say noon. That will give you some time to think about what you saw and perhaps be a little calmer. How about meeting at the Visitor Center, I'll wear a red shirt and jeans so you can recognize me. Do you mind if I record our conversation, I'm still working on that article I mentioned on my web site?"

"Oh, thank you so much" I said, "next Saturday would be great. No, I don't mind you recording our conversation; I should be much calmer by then. My friend who was with me who also saw the ghosts doesn't want anything to do with this, so she won't be with me. Again, thank you so much for meeting me, I am just so excited! I'll see you next Saturday" and I hung up the phone.

He must think I'm a total idiot, but he did agree to meet me. I was floating on cloud nine. I need to make a list of questions like what was it like living then, what did they wear and eat and how did they survive all the sickness that went around then and, does he know anything about the 63rd Ohio, and...oh, now I'm really rambling, I need to settle down. So I sat down at my desk and made a detailed listing of the questions I wanted to ask the Professor.

Feeling much better after I got my thoughts somewhat in order, I went to see Jane. I knocked on her door, "Jane, may I come in."

"Not if you want to talk about ghosts" she said.

"No, I want to talk about the party Tuesday night that I promised you I would go to with you."

Jane opened her door, smiling, and said "Well if that's the case, come on in."

I sat down on her bed and asked her if she was doing OK after yesterday. She said that she was and started telling me about Tuesday's party. "Everyone who is anyone will be there. You have to wear a black dress, black extra high heels and pearls if you want to impress anyone there. And we can't get there until 9:00 pm, so don't plan on getting a lot of sleep that night, we're going to *partee*!"

Oh great, I really hate parties, but I smiled and said I couldn't wait to go with her.

Next I went to see Janet. I told her about my meeting next Saturday with the Professor. She said,

"Do you suppose it's safe to meet him there, he could be a pervert for all you know."

I told her that he seemed like a nice older gentleman and that I was really looking forward to meeting him and to learn more about 'our' ghosts, and that I was sure it was safe in such a public place. She did make me promise to call her if anything did not seem on the up-and-up. She then reminded me that I had promised to go to the Atlanta History Center with her on Wednesday. I told her I would love to, as I was thinking to myself that I was going to be out late Tuesday and now Wednesday, I hope I can survive both days and work my normal 50 hours this week.

I did my normal Sunday chores and turned in early, hoping to catch up on a little sleep that I knew I would not be getting Tuesday and Wednesday. Hope my little black dress still fits!

Chapter 9

Monday was a good day at work; I only had to work 8 ½ hours instead of my normal 10. I thought about the ghosts about a hundred times, but I said nothing of them to my co-workers. I knew they would scoff or just plain call me crazy. I couldn't wait to get home to do some more research on Kennesaw Mountain.

I opened the front door to my home and called out "Anyone home?" No one answered; there was a note on the kitchen counter that Barbara was called out on a flight to Hawaii and would not be home until Wednesday. Tough duty I thought, as I rummaged in the refrigerator for some cheese and finding some fruit on the counter decided this would be dinner for tonight.

I headed to my bedroom, changed into some comfy sweats and turned on my trusty computer. I searched for sites on Kennesaw Mountain and scrolled down to one that looked interesting.

I learned a lot on just that one web site. For one thing, I discovered that on the day of the major battle there, June 27, 1864, it was 100 degrees. How did they survive just the weather? I also learned some pretty bizarre facts, like because of the heat, the wounded men lay on the battlefield for many hours and their wounds became infested with maggots – gross!

Over 5,350 soldiers who were killed in the battle fought in that campaign from June 19, 1864 through July 2, 1864.

Sherman was a redhead like me!

Daniel McCook who led the assault at Cheatham Hill was from Ohio and shared a law office with none other than the infamous General William Tecumseh Sherman. Daniel McCook died from his wounds in this battle.

Today, visitors can explore this battlefield, thanks in part to the foresight of Lansing J. Dawdy, an Illinois veteran of the battle. In 1899 Dawdy purchased sixty acres of land near the Dead Angle. The property was transferred in 1904 to the Kennesaw Mountain Battlefield Association.

I looked at about 30 different websites. I looked up at the clock and it was 8:00 pm when I heard the front door open. Janet and Jane were home so I turned off the computer and went down to visit them.

"Hi guys" I said, "how was your day."

Janet said, "Long!"

Jane said, "It was good."

So much for small talk, I thought. I told them that Barbara had been called out on a flight and would not be back until Wednesday.

Jane, always the bubbly one, said "Make sure you're ready to leave at 8:30 tomorrow night. Let me look at you to make sure you pass inspection though first. I'll drive because I know where the party is taking place and also because I don't want you sneaking out earlier than I'm ready to go; you do owe me you know."

I knew I was never going to live Saturday down! "OK, fine" I said, "but that line is going to get old really fast. I said I would go with you to the party, regardless of the fact that we saw ghosts you know. I'm turning in early so I meet your inspection tomorrow night. Goodnight all."

Chapter 10

Tuesday was a killer of a day at work; guess they were making up for my nice short day on Monday. I didn't leave the office until 6:30 p.m. and did not get home until 7:30 p.m.

Jane met me at the door in a panic. "I thought you were going to rat out on me and not show up! I would never have forgiven you, and now I'm all a nervous wreck and it's all your fault!"

"Whoa, whoa!" I said, "I just had to work late. Let me go get a shower and chill out for a minute and then you can check my appearance to make sure I pass muster, OK?"

I ran up the stairs and shut my bedroom door. I sat down on the bed and breathed deeply. This evening is not going to go well, I can tell, I thought to myself. Oh well, nothing I can do but try to look my best. I stripped and jumped in the shower. After a long hot shower I felt much better and actually began to look forward to the evening.

I reached in the closet for my perfect black dress and my three-inch platform heels. *Don't forget the pearls*, I thought and rummaged for them in my jewelry box. I added pearl earrings, sprayed on my best perfume and walked to the mirror. Not bad I thought, maybe this evening won't be so bad after all.

I walked to Jane's room. She was tearing her closet apart. "What's up?" I asked.

"I can't find my midnight blue dress, help me will ya?"

I went to her closet and reached for the dress with no problem and handed it her. "What has you in such a dither?" I asked.

"OK, it's like this. I heard Brad, the most eligible bachelor in Atlanta is going to be there and I definitely want to look my best. I've heard he is a super nice guy too, for a rich dude. I've been dying to meet him and I'm really nervous, that's why I really wanted you to be there with me for moral support."

She got out her high heels and put them on. "And besides all that, I'm really afraid I'm going to end up an old maid and I just can't stand that." She sniffled a little and I went over and put my arms around her.

"You're not going to end up an old maid, I promise. Now finish getting ready and let's go make an entrance!"

We put on our wraps and walked out of the house, arm in arm to her 2010 green Jeep. *I hope this guy doesn't get a look at her car* I thought, as we got in and backed out of our driveway.

Chapter 11

We arrived at a real honest to goodness mansion. The driveway was a half mile long. The house must have been at least 15,000 square feet with a six-car garage. There was a small carriage house behind the main house, a large swimming pool and what looked like a pool house too. The house was ablaze with lights and people were everywhere.

"Whose house is this" I asked?

"I don't know their name, somebody on the Atlanta Falcon's football team is all I heard from my friend who wrangled us the invitations" answered Jane. I thought that football players worked really hard but were extremely overpaid and must not know what to do with all the money they made.

"OK, I'm going to mingle and look for Brad, are you alright on your own?" Jane asked.

"Yeah, I'm OK, go on. If I don't see you in two hours I'll call you on your cell phone, you do have it on you, don't you?" I asked.

"Yes, I do, see you later alligator!" and off she went into the crowd.

There were 60" TV's in every room. I saw what looked liked fine Persian rugs on the wooden floors. There were six 12' white pillars in the living room that looked like they weighed 1,000 pounds each.

People were everywhere, mostly mingling in small groups. I knew no one so I headed for the bar and ordered a glass of White Zinfandel. I looked for the food and found a large table with food I'm sure I could not even have pronounced let alone knew what it was. I picked up a few things that looked good.

I crossed the room to a large bookcase and pursued the vast leather-bound volumes as I nibbled on the little delicacies on my plate. Shakespeare, Hemingway, Voltaire were among the many authors. I spied a large book and saw that it was on the Civil War. It was 'Decision in the West' by Albert Castel. It was about the Atlanta Campaign, I learned, as I began leafing my way through its chapters and pages, looking for the Battle of Kennesaw Mountain.

I felt his deep blue eyes on me before I saw him, this tall man looking down at me, looking over my shoulder. He must have been well over six feet tall, the jet black wavy hair combed neatly back, the wide smile on his strong, tanned face quickly changed to an expression of slight embarrassment as he stepped back from me.

"Hi, please excuse me...I was just trying to see what you were so engrossed in. Most people come to a party to talk, not look at books."

I stammered a little and said "Hi, I don't know anyone here except my roommate so I was looking for something to keep my interest. My name is Kathleen Kelley, what's yours?"

"Pleased to meet you Kathleen...that's a fine Irish name. I'm Roger Barnes. I'm a neighbor and the only people I know here is the owner of this house, Kevin Charles. I see you were looking at a Civil War book, is that something that interests you? I've recently become interested in the subject too. My great-great grandfather was a Corporal in the 63rd Ohio Volunteer Infantry, Company C, and I've just received a chest of his that my father had inherited and now has come to me."

My mouth came open and I just stared at him. I didn't know what to say, I was truly speechless. How could our ancestors both have been Corporals in the same unit from Ohio? Was someone or something guiding me to my destiny; were they leading me to see things and meet people that were to affect my life forever? I was beginning to wonder seriously if this might be the case.

"Careful, you'll catch a fly in that pretty opened mouth of yours. Did I say something wrong?"

All I could do was look at him. What could I say that wouldn't sound idiotic?

"No, no, nothing's wrong," I replied, still slightly holding my breath. I know I was still staring at him and I know he was wondering why.

"Nothing's wrong, but shocking, bordering on unbelievable. I don't know how to explain it just now, it's just so beyond coincidence."

The wide smile returned. "I've got all night, how about you" he asked with that wonderfully deep and melodiously seductive voice.

"OK, let's go find a place to sit down and talk," I said.

But first, how about a glass of wine? I thought to myself and led us to the bar. I ordered my second and last glass of wine for the evening and he ordered a scotch and water. I headed for the entertainment room in the back of the house and found a fairly empty room. I sat down in the first empty chair I found and Roger sat down next to me.

I smiled at him and said "Tell me a little bit about yourself, like where are you from, if you're not from here how did you get to Atlanta?"

"Well, I'm originally from Akron, Ohio. My parents and I moved to Atlanta when I was sixteen. I went to Georgia Tech and graduated in Electrical Engineering. I work for the largest engineering firm in Atlanta and I'm an only child. I lived with my parents next door until they died last year. Now it's just me and my dog, Kahlua, in that rambling monstrosity, a lot like this one. Tell me a little about yourself."

I sipped my wine, took a deep breath and began. "I'm originally from Columbus, Ohio; I too am an only child. I moved here two years ago with my best friends Janet, Jane and Barbara. We share a house in Buckhead. I came to the party with Jane, she's here somewhere. What so surprised me earlier was that you had an ancestor in the 63rd Ohio Volunteer Infantry. I too had an ancestor in that unit, also in Company C and he was also a Corporal. He also had two younger brothers who were in the same unit, they were both privates. We're both from Ohio and both the only child of our parents. Don't you think that is a lot of coincidence, all in the space of about 10 minutes?"

"Well", Roger said, "First of all, I don't believe in coincidence. But I do believe in destiny. Perhaps destiny has drawn us together for a reason.

What do you think about that?" He had an interesting smirk on his face and I couldn't help but think how attractive he was. *I had been thinking on a similar line since I met you,* I thought, but did not say so. "Could I ask you another question" I asked.

"Sure go ahead" he said.

"Do you believe in ghosts?"

"Well, I've never seen one but I do believe in the unexplained."

I think I've heard that before, isn't that what Jane had said, I wondered? "I saw four of them at Kennesaw Mountain just yesterday and I think they may have something to do with the 63rd Ohio or they were saying something to me specifically, I think. The strange thing is that Jane saw them at the same time I did. I'm just not sure at this point, but next Saturday I'm meeting a Professor who has been researching paranormal activities at different Civil War battle sites. He also saw the ghosts we saw at the exact same place that we did. Would you like to go with me?"

He thought a few seconds and said "I would like that very much Kathleen. I'd also like to learn more about you. I think our destinies may be entwined and I can't wait to find out where miss destiny leads us next."

My heart skipped several beats. I reached in my bag, found a piece of paper and a pen and wrote down my phone number. "Here's my number, I told the Professor I would meet him at the Kennesaw Mountain visitor center at noon this Saturday. Can you meet me there?"

We agreed to meet there and he said he had to go to take Kahlua on her nightly walk. He kissed me lightly on my cheek and walked out of the room.

I swooned a little over Roger's brief kiss and thought over the strange events of the evening. Then I went looking for Jane. I eventually found her along with a large crowd at the food area. "It's 11:30pm, you about ready to go girlfriend?" I asked.

She said yes and "Did you have a great time, I really had a great time and I talked to Brad and we're going out next Saturday and I'm really tired and ready to go home. Did you meet anyone interesting?"

I said that I had; I couldn't think of what I could tell her and my strange encounter with Roger so I said nothing more and we went in search of our wraps.

Jane was all excited as we departed the house and headed for her Jeep. "I had just a great time, thanks for coming with me Kath."

I thought that I had an interesting evening too, but I think it was more than just a great time, but time would tell. "Yeah it was great, but I'm tired now and that Wednesday morning alarm is going to be ringing way earlier than I'm ready for it."

The drive home was short since there was not much traffic on the roads. I let us in the front door, told Jane goodnight and headed to my bedroom. I undressed, got ready for bed and laid down for probably a six-hour sleep at best. As I drifted off to sleep my last thoughts were on Roger, our conversation, and that sweet kiss.

Chapter 12

I groaned and turned off the alarm; 6:00am and another long day, I thought. Tonight was the Atlanta History Center with Janet. I was looking forward to this trip though I wanted to research more about Kennesaw Mountain while Janet looked for her ancestors.

I showered and dressed for work. I grabbed a quick cup of coffee and headed out the door, sensing that I was the only one in the house. It seemed lonely to me...it was seldom that I was the only one there. I briefly thought of last night's party, of Roger and of this coming Saturday. I wondered what I would discover, both about Professor Wilcox and about Roger. And of course, about those ghosts!

My boss was out of town so the day was quiet and I got a lot accomplished. When I cleared everything from my desk that needed completed I looked at the clock and saw that it was exactly 5:00 p.m. and I was ready to head out the door. I grabbed my purse, pulled out my car keys and headed for the parking deck.

This week was truly one of firsts; I had attended my first party in Atlanta, met an amazingly gorgeous man who I sensed would lead me to many new adventures, seen my first ghost and left the office for the first time after only working 8 hours. Life was good!

Traffic was light and I pulled in my driveway at 5:30. I opened the door, threw my keys on the hallway table and headed for the kitchen to the amazing aroma of dinner cooking.

Barbara and Janet were busy cooking a delicious-smelling chicken stir-fry. "Hi guys, what's the occasion of you two cooking dinner? How was your flight to Hawaii Barbara?"

"Wanted to get dinner done so we can get to the History Center soon" said Janet.

"And the flight was great" Barbara said. Janet served us and we hurriedly ate.

"This is really good guys, thanks." I helped clean up the dishes and ran to my room to change.

"OK Janet, let's go, it should only take us about 15 minutes to get there, I'll drive" I said. We hurriedly left and arrived at the Center in 17 minutes, pretty good for Atlanta traffic.

The Keenan Research Center is housed on the bottom floor of the History Center. I had been there once before so I led the way. We signed in at the desk and checked our purses and coats in the locker they assigned to us.

The library houses about 33,000 books, manuscripts and photographs, and can be a little daunting when you first go there. You can research online so I already knew the books that Janet would want to look at and knew where the Civil War section was also. I led Janet to the area she needed, told her where I was going and to meet me there when she was through, and then headed to the history section.

I immediately went to the book *"Kennesaw Mountain, June 1864: Bitter standoff at the Gibraltar of Georgia"* by Richard A. Baumgartner and Larry M. Strayer. I looked through the book for quite awhile and copied several pages to take home and read.

I found 19 other books, looked through them all and copied some from each one. When I looked at my watch is was already 8:00pm, so I went in search of Janet.

Reading about the terrible hardships on both sides as well as the hardships of the people just trying to get by made me very sad. War is hell, just as Sherman said.

Janet was still looking at census records. She excitedly said "I found my great-great grandparents. They emigrated from Germany to New York, moved to Ohio and lived there for thirty years. They moved after that to St. Louis, Missouri...I never knew that."

"That's great news, now you have somewhere to start from to find out lots more. It's 8:45 and time to go home" I said.

We gathered our belongings from the locker and were home in fifteen minutes. "I'm bushed" I said, "It's an early night for me."

"Thanks for going with me tonight" Janet said. "See you tomorrow!"

Just before I went to sleep I thought of Roger and wondered why he had not called. I was very busy this week, so maybe he was too. I was looking forward to seeing him on Saturday.

Chapter 13

Roger Barnes was not looking forward to another restless night with little sleep; another restless night of trying to make up his mind whether he wanted to call that cute, red-haired girl with the Irish name who decided to look at a history book instead of mix and mingle and party the other night.

He was burned out on false starts, on relationships that he hoped with all his heart would lead somewhere but ended up, at best, nowhere, and at worst, painful.

Could this be the beginning of another one, he wondered, or could she maybe be the one? But hell, there's nothing there yet, just a date to meet at a Civil War battlefield north of Atlanta, a shared interest based on sheer coincidence, although he had chosen at that moment to call it destiny. And while he did not want to admit it to Kathleen Kelley, he did believe in coincidence as well as destiny. And that is where she seemed different.

He felt he had been a bit forward with her at the party, kissing a woman he had never seen before on the cheek, even if it was a discreet, polite gesture, almost like kissing your sister, but he couldn't have stopped himself if he had thought about it for an hour, it was something he just had to do.

But she did not seem to mind. Was she wondering why he had not called after she gave him her phone number....it's getting kind of late, maybe I better not.

Oh, to hell with it....He dialed the number, a sleepy voice answered.

"Hello," it said.

"Oh, hi, Kathleen, it's Roger, Roger Barnes, from the other night at the party. Hey I'm sorry, I didn't realize what time it was, you sound like you were asleep. I am so, so sorry, I'll call back tomorrow and much earlier."

The deep rich voice on the phone captured her attention from the first word and she was not about to let him go.

"NO! no, no, Roger, it's o.k., its o.k., I was asleep but I'm wide awake now. I've had two late nights this week and I turned in early. I'm so glad to hear from you, I'm in bed, but that's all right, don't worry about the time, guess where I've spent the day?"

"Do I get three guesses and the first two don't count?" he laughed.

"Silly," I laughed back. "I've been to the Atlanta History Center down on West Paces Ferry Road, absolutely fascinating place, and I found a lot of information on Kennesaw Mountain, it was really fascinating. There were twenty books in all and I copied quite a bit from each one of them. I wanted to ask you what all you know about your ancestor that fought in the 63rd Ohio; what do you know about him, do you have census data, or his Civil War record, or any other information?"

"No, like I said I just started looking for details on him, and then I have this chest of his, I have done no research on his military history and I've never looked at a census record in my life. I do want to know all about him, just haven't had the time. Can you tell me where to begin?"

"I'd like to help you and that way I'll learn more about the 63rd and my ancestor too. I've accumulated some books on the war, and I recently found and copied one called *"Fuller's Ohio Brigade."* The 63rd was part of Fuller's Brigade. But, like you, I really haven't had time. Now I want to make the time and learn all I can about them and about the Atlanta Campaign of the Civil War because the 63rd fought in it and my ancestors did too. But more importantly, I want to know why I saw those ghosts at Kennesaw Mountain. Maybe I'll learn something from Professor Wilcox that will help me to understand."

"I'm looking forward to going to Kennesaw with you on Saturday, Kathleen" Roger said. "But now, I need to get to bed myself, sorry I woke you, I'll see you on Saturday...goodnight."

"Goodnight Roger, I'm looking forward to seeing you too." I hung up the phone and snuggled deeply into my pillow and wondered what Saturday would bring.

After Roger got ready for bed he sat in his favorite chair, smoking his favorite pipe and wondered where, if anywhere, this relationship would go. He had a sneaking suspicion that perhaps destiny really was involved.

Chapter 14

I dragged home from work at 7:30 p.m. on Thursday night. There was a major wreck on the freeway and it took me forever to get home. Atlanta traffic was the only thing I hated about this town.

Barbara greeted me in the kitchen. "What took you so long girl?"

"Just this god-awful traffic" I said. "What have you been up to lately, I haven't seen you much."

"I've been working a lot! Filling in for some stews that have had the flu...in fact I go out at 7:00 a.m. tomorrow for Seattle. Weather has delayed a lot of flights the last couple of weeks too. I met a stupendilicious male on my last flight and I have a date with him Saturday night. He actually lives here but he travels a lot. I've seen him about four times on different flights out of Atlanta. His name is Ryan and he is an attorney for a major company based out of Atlanta. He is a gorgeous hunk of man; six foot three, blond hair, green eyes and guess where he's from?"

"Gee, I can't imagine, where" I said.

"His family is from Chester, Ohio, can you believe it. He's 30 so you probably don't know him. He's been in Atlanta for six years now, he's never been married and he is just so sweet. We're going to a movie early and then dinner after, I just can't wait."

Well, I thought to myself, everyone is meeting handsome men lately, maybe the moon is just right. "I met a nice guy at the party Jane and I went to also. His name is Roger and I'm meeting him at Kennesaw

Mountain on Saturday. Seems we both have a date on Saturday."

"Where is everyone else?" I asked.

"Jane and Janet went to a movie tonight, they'll probably be in late. I've got to get to bed early since I have to get up so early, so I probably won't see you until Sunday. Enjoy your day with Roger!"

"Night" I said and headed to my bedroom.

I turned on my computer and saw an article about movie stars seeing ghosts in their homes. I figured most of them had older homes, well mansions not homes, and wondered why I was seeing so much about ghosts all of a sudden. Was it an omen I wondered, or was it just something that had been going on and I had just not noticed?

I once again looked up ghosts. I discovered that in the South, people called ghosts 'haints'. I had never heard that before, so I looked up the definition. It was not in the dictionary, but according to the website haint is a southern expression for a ghost, apparition or spirit. Other colloquialisms for haints include boogers, goblins and spooks. Shades of blue, in the southern U.S were called "haint blue," a popular paint color for houses and rooms to keep spirits away. Doors and window shutters, both used to block entrance to the home, are commonly painted in shades of blue by the superstitious.

Then I looked up the definition of ghost and it said "In traditional belief, a ghost is the soul or spirit of a deceased person or animal that can appear, in visible form or other manifestation, to the living." The

Scottish called them 'wraith', and almost every country has a different name for them.

One website I found said that people visiting the area would see soldiers on the battlefield and hear screams and gun shots. Recently people have seen entire groups of soldiers and thought a Civil War reenactment was going on. Housing subdivisions have been built on part of the battlefield and people have seen the ghosts of Civil War soldiers walking in their houses and yards. Many paranormal investigators have investigated the site and say the area is a hot bed of paranormal activity. I'll have to ask the Professor about all this.

Chapter 15

Roger Barnes was sitting in his office on Peachtree Street working on a request for a quote when he heard his friends, Mike and Steve, in a heated discussion about ghosts. That got his attention, so he put down his pen and walked over to Mike's office. "What's up guys? Did I hear you talking about ghosts?"

Mike said that he was at Kennesaw Mountain last Sunday and had seen the ghost of a Union soldier at the Dead Angle, just a few yards from where he was standing with his wife, Dawn. He said one minute the soldier was there and the next minute he was gone. His wife had not seen the ghost and had kidded him about it ever since. Steve said he did not believe in ghosts and that Mike must be getting muddled in the head in his old age.

He told them about Kathleen and her having seen ghosts there just the day before, so there must really be something going on there. They were still arguing when he headed back to his desk.

He tried getting back to the quote but kept thinking about ghosts. He'd never seen one and never really given the subject much thought. Then he thought maybe coincidence was not the right word for what was going on, there were just too many people who have seen them. He decided to do some research of his own on ghosts, and was really looking forward to meeting this Professor Wilcox that Kathleen had mentioned. He was glad that it was Friday and he would be meeting him tomorrow.

He gave up getting back to work since it was already 4:30 p.m. so he cleaned up his desk and headed out the door. He was meeting his best friends Josh and Cody at 7:00 p.m. for dinner, so he headed home, got a shower, walked Kahlua, and then drove to the restaurant where they were to meet.

Chapter 16

Charles Wilcox was up late, sitting in his overstuffed recliner, a birthday present years ago from Mamie, studying his notes about the hot sultry struggle that occurred on a ridge at the center of the Confederate line nearly 150 years ago, and his place and circumstance there. Memories began to flood in to haunt him, and to comfort him. Tonight he wanted to rest and remember. Tomorrow he would wear a red shirt so the young woman from Ohio, Kathleen Kelley, would see him and recognize him, and he would share those notes, those recollections with her, but tonight, he just wanted to remember.

It was a hot June day that he saw them, as he recalled, it was June 27th, the very day of the battle, when Thomas hurled his Army of the Cumberland brigades of Illinois and Ohio men and boys against, most considered, the best soldiers of the Army of Tennessee, the divisions of the Tennessee horseman Ben Cheatham and the Irishman from Arkansas, Patrick Cleburne.

He had been there many times before, stood on the ground at the Angle, and knew in his heart and mind what happened there. For him, the battle still lived, the vision of his thoughts took him back to that day, that morning, that hour, when those men in dirty dark blue tried in vain to end the fight for Atlanta.

So was it that knowledge, and the vision it brought, that made them appear, those four men of the Union, with their bayonets fixed, gritty determination on their faces, as he saw them on the crest of the earth works at the Angle? Or was it the feeling he had experienced so many times at re-enactment events when he was portraying combat, either as a Federal or Rebel... that he was really there, that he had gone back in time and for an instant, he had let go of reality?

But he saw them, saw them clearly; they appeared to be coming right at him, savage, full of the rage of battle and the irresistible urge to kill the enemy, knowing that if they failed, they certainly would die. He could not believe what he was seeing, but they were there and he was there and he stepped back, staring in horror and fear, and as suddenly as they appeared, they were gone. Had he seen some kind of replay, had some kind of window in time opened at that very spot at that very moment and the soldiers came through it?

He went home to Mamie...he had to share what he had seen with her. She had listened patiently, seeing he was serious and that this was not one of his little pranks, and then she smiled.

"Honey, you get so deep into your impression sometimes, and history lives for you so much, I'm not surprised you haven't seen something like this up there way before now. I believe you Charlie! I believe you saw what you saw even though it's incredible. Tell you what, let's go up there tomorrow and let's see what I see."

The following day Mamie and Charlie stood at the Angle, it was Saturday, there were other people there, with children, some genuinely interested in the history of the place, most just there to get out of the house and go outdoors for the day, jogging, walking their pet dogs, with no interest or concern about what had happened at Cheatham Hill.

"This is where I saw them," Charlie said, turning to Mamie, who for a long moment, stared at the crest of the breast works, concentrating.

"It was blood and destruction that day, wasn't it darling," she said. "I can just imagine what happened here, but Charlie, I don't see anything. Tell you the truth, this is an eerie place, and if there was any place around that ought to be haunted, this would be it, so many young men dying with their lives still ahead of them, so many with unresolved issues I expect. I've read that's what causes people to come back from the dead and haunt a place. Sorry Sweetie, I just don't see your charging Yankees."

Why is it that some see them, and some don't, Charles wondered, as he pondered the memory of that day. Why did I see them, and Mamie, so close to me in mind and spirit, did not? Why have others seen them at different times, all describing the same thing, the same foursome charging on the breast work, muskets fixed with bayonets ready to kill or be killed. Why did Kathleen Kelley see them, her only link to the place being her war ancestry? Why?

Tomorrow, maybe, finally, he would find out tomorrow, but tonight he would let the thought of Mamie's sweetness from that day and all the other days and years with her sooth him. He fell asleep in his recliner.

Chapter 17

I woke up early Saturday morning, excited about what the day would bring. I was really looking forward to seeing both the Professor and Roger. I looked out the window, it was just getting light; the weather man had predicted a 50 degree day with lots of sunshine and I was thankful for a nice day to be walking around Kennesaw Mountain.

Once again after I turned onto Old U.S. 41 off Barrett Parkway I had the sense of going back, going back and away from the present day; of four lane highways and fast food restaurants and convenience store gas stations that populated the Parkway.

As soon as I made the turn, all that went away, there was nothing but woodland, bare, gray and haunting this time of year, but with March, the beginning of the promise of new life with the arrival of spring.

I turned into the entrance and parked, and saw the red shirt before its owner saw me. He was a studious but friendly looking man, balding, with hair and beard that had long since turned gray, and under his right arm was a manila folder thick with what I guessed was reference material.

I walked up to him and smiled. "Professor Wilcox, I presume. How do you do, I'm Kathleen Kelley. It's so nice to meet you in person."

Charlie looked at the young woman from Ohio for a long moment and almost wept, but did not, and gave her his warmest smile instead. My God, how she looks like Mamie when we first met so long ago, he thought. She had the same stature, the same bright green eyes, and the same sweet smile. If God had blessed us with a daughter this is how she would have looked, I think. He hoped she did not notice his stare and hurriedly replied.

"The pleasure is mine Kathleen, truly it is, how lovely it is to see such a young pretty woman on such a day when winter's chill is still in the air."

"I'm impressed, I have an intellectual, and a historian with southern charm to teach me about Kennesaw Mountain," Kathleen said, blushing slightly. "I haven't told you yet, but someone else is meeting us here too, I hope you don't mind. His name is Roger Barnes and I met him just a week ago at a party. Coincidentally, or not perhaps, but he has an ancestor in the 63rd OVI just like I do and he is interested in learning more about him too, so I suggested he join us today."

"I don't mind at all" Charlie said, "I always enjoy teaching people about history, and especially Civil War history that occurred right here. Would you like a drink while we wait on him?"

"No thanks" Kathleen said, "I brought along a bottle of water with me."

Just then Roger pulled up next to them and jauntily hopped out of his car. "Good morning Kathleen and I guess this has to be the professor you told me about. Good morning sir" as he offered a polite handshake. "And good morning to you too Kath, I'm really glad to see you today."

Kathleen blushed again, and said "Hi".

"All right you young people," said the Professor, "Please call me Pappy, most everyone does. Where would you like to begin our talk?"

Kathleen looked around and seeing a bench shaded by a large tree said, "Let's sit there, if that's OK with everyone."

They moved to the bench and sat down. Pappy began, "Let me tell you a little about my background and how I came to study ghosts."

"I began Civil War reenacting a long time ago, back in 1980 when I first moved to the West side of Atlanta. I enjoyed the hobby, the camaraderie with the other re-enactors; I'll admit I also enjoyed the shooting of the guns and the taking of prisoners. But along the way, I started really being interested in the history of that war, the places where it occurred, and the people who lived and died in it."

"Are you guys bored yet?" and both Kathleen and Roger said "On, no, tell us more."

"Well, the more I learned and the more battlefields I walked on, the more ghosts I began to see. At first I was so taken aback that I didn't even admit seeing them to myself. It happens so quickly, the mind almost can't process the sighting I've found."

"I saw my first one at Gettysburg, the second at Antietam and the most I've seen have been right here at Kennesaw Mountain. I've seen a few others along the way too. I started talking to others who had experiences, and believe me there are more than you would think. Then I began documenting my experiences along with many, many other people, and here I am now with a 750 page research paper. It's become a popular topic, I'm sure you've probably seen the many TV shows about hauntings and ghosts. In the beginning, most people wouldn't say much, guess it was kind of taboo and people were kind of skittish about the subject, but in the last fifteen years you hear more and more."

"Why don't we go ahead and drive over to Cheatham Hill, I can talk more while we're on the way" Pappy said.

Roger and I got in his car, pulled out of the Park and Pappy began again, "There are different types of ghost sightings. One is like here at Kennesaw Mountain. Traumatic events may leave an impression like a tape recorder. The scene plays over and over. Cold and dampness also seem to play a factor. Also, people report seeing more ghosts in the winter than in the summer. There also may be an electromagnetic field which is stronger in some areas than others. You might be interested in the fact that Stonehenge has a large magnetic field too, and people have been seeing things there for centuries. Then there are hauntings. In hauntings, people tend to see the same image or ghost repeat the same thing over and over, say like someone always seeing a ghost walk up the stairway. Some ghosts seem to be able to move from place to place, even from one house to another house.

There are several organizations that deal with this type of phenomena. There is even one right here in Georgia called the Psychical Research Foundation located in Carrollton, Georgia. They would be a good group to contact if you want further information."

We drove up the long drive and parked at the parking lot for Cheatham Hill. We all got out of the car and Pappy explained about the area. We walked from the parking lot to the area known as the Dead Angle. Pappy suggested we all walk around, not together but separately, and get a feel for the area. "Think about what happened here almost a hundred and fifty years ago. Think about the soldiers, the heat; remember it was 100 degrees on the day of the battle, so the men were suffering; some did not have enough water, they were far from home, fighting for what they believed was right. Most of them were very young...18-22 was the average age. Let's meet in front of the Illinois Monument in fifteen minutes" finished Pappy and we all walked off in different directions.

I walked back toward the parking area, just looking off into the wooded area to my left, thinking about what Pappy had said about the day the battle was fought. How could boys who were dressed in wool, toting 50 pounds or more have survived in that heat? I just could not fathom my doing that, I probably would not have survived a day, let alone four years.

It was once again eerily quiet; there were not many people in the area, and even the birds were not singing. I looked at my watch and decided I had better head back in order to meet up with Pappy and Roger in the allotted time.

I saw Roger up ahead at the area of the Dead Angle. He bent down and picked something up, I couldn't tell what it was from that distance. When I finally walked up to him he was white as a ghost and had a glazed, far-away look in his eye.

"Hi Roger, I saw you pick something up, what did you find?"

He looked at me like I was from outer space or something, kind of shook his head a little and opened his mouth to speak but nothing came out.

"Roger, are you OK?" I took his arm because he looked like he might faint.

He shook my arm off, shook his head again and said "I really thought you were a little wacko when we first met and you talked about seeing ghosts here, but now I know if you are, then so am I. Let's go find Pappy so I can tell you together what happened to me."

I looked up at him, wondering if he too had seen the ghost, but I said nothing per his request. I took a hold of his arm and followed him to where Pappy was standing in front of the Illinois monument. Pappy looked up as we approached and searched our faces, I guess wondering what our experiences had been.

Roger spoke first. "I came here today thinking this was nothing more than a nice day to walk around an historical area. I also came thinking that both you and Kathleen were a little crazy thinking you had seen ghosts here, but now I know you both spoke the truth. I was walking in the area of the Dead Angle when my shoe bumped something. I looked down and there was a bullet...a Civil War era bullet! I bent over and picked it up. I thought about what you said, about what had happened here so many years ago. I thought about my ancestor who had walked on this very ground, and that's when it happened. I looked up at the area where the Confederates had lain in wait for the Union forces, and I saw one soldier, a Confederate soldier. He was lying in the ditch there with his rifle aimed right at me, and then in a fraction of a second he was gone. I will never say never again because I saw with my own eyes something I believed was impossible to see, a ghost!"

Pappy patted Roger's shoulder and said, "I know exactly how you feel son, it has happened to me the same way. Like I said, it happens so fast that you question whether you even saw what you think you saw, but trust me, you did see something."

"I thought the same as you too" said Kathleen.

"Let me take a look at that bullet Roger" said Pappy.

Roger handed it to him and Pappy looked it over. "This is a rare find these days Roger, most people don't ever find a bullet on Federal land anymore. You know we have to take this and hand it over to the Ranger here. It's against the law to keep anything found on this property. Let's head back to the park and see Willie."

We walked back to the car and drove to the park, no one spoke on the way back, it had been quite a day again here at Kennesaw Mountain. I wondered if something would happen to me every time I came here, or if perhaps I would never see another ghost in my life. Time would tell I guess.

We walked into the park office and asked for Willie. They told us he was in the museum but would be back in just a minute so we waited. He arrived in just a few minutes, saw us and said, "Hello there, aren't you the young lady that was here just a couple of weeks ago?"

I said yes, that I had been here earlier. Roger went up to him and handed over the bullet.

"I believe this is park property sir, I found it at Cheatham Hill just a little while ago, at the Dead Angle."

Willie took it and said "We don't get many people handing these over; I'm not sure if there just aren't many more out there or if people just don't turn them in, but I really thank you for being honest and bringing this one to me. We'll display it with the others we have. You know, where you were at the Dead Angle, people used to find thousands of items like this; bullets, belt buckles, breast plates, even parts of muskets in the trenches. It was a treasure trove of battlefield artifacts until it became Federal property."

"How much do you think is still out there" Roger asked?

"I really don't know" Willie said, "keep in mind there is a lot of battlefield off park property, and sometimes when there is construction, artifacts are uncovered. You held a piece of history in your hand young man. You might want to remember that."

We bid Willie good day and left the museum and headed for our cars. "I'm starved, what do you think about getting some lunch" Roger asked Kathleen and Pappy.

"Sounds good to me, there is a Red Lobster just a couple blocks up the road" said Kathleen.

"OK with me, said Pappy."

We headed to our cars and drove the short distance.

Chapter 18

Roger arrived first, then Pappy and then Kathleen.

"Lunch is on me" said Roger "since today is my lucky day; I saw a ghost and found a Civil War bullet."

After a brief wait, the trio were escorted to a corner booth and ordered drinks. Roger, although he said he was hungry, had the battlefield on his mind. "I feel like I've had a life-changing experience" he told Kathleen and Pappy, while they all looked over the menu.

Kathleen looked up and looked Roger right in the eyes "Don't you wish we could go back in time to a few days before the battle and talk to our ancestors and see what life was really like for them?"

Roger smiled, his eyes full of excitement "You bet" he replied, "but we wouldn't just be talking to them if we went back in time, we would be part of what they were involved in."

The waitress appeared and asked if they were ready to order and all three said, "No, give us a few more minutes please."

The waitress said, "That's fine, no problem, take your time", with a slight bit of irritation in her voice. When she left their table Kathleen said, "Guess she wants us to order soon...must need us to hurry up so she can get her tip quota for the day."

They all looked over the menu and all decided to get a shrimp platter. The waitress came back, got their orders and then hurried off to turn it in to the cook.

"You know, I've often thought about going back in time myself to experience that day at the Dead Angle. It would have been terrible, but then unlike you two, it has never occurred to me to go back a few days before the battle. Still, a time traveler would have to become part of his surroundings or the people of that time would not relate to him, would they?" said Pappy.

"Now I can't wait to see what's in that trunk that my ancestor left me" said Roger.

He then told Pappy all about his ancestor and that he had been left a trunk of his. "I don't think Mom or Dad even looked in that trunk, they sure never mentioned it to me" Roger said. "It may never have seen daylight for almost a hundred and fifty years" Roger said out loud, more to himself than to the others. "Kath, you just have to follow me home today so we can go through the trunk together, I just can't wait even another day."

It seemed so important now, after what had happened today, so Kathleen agreed to follow him and check out the mysterious contents of the trunk.

Pappy said "Please call me and let me know what you find, now you have my curiosity peaked!"

Lunch arrived and they hurriedly ate their delicious shrimp. Roger left the waitress a good tip and they all left the restaurant.

"I really enjoyed this day" said Pappy.

"Thank you for going with us Pappy and telling us all you did about ghosts and the battle" said Kathleen.

"Thank you so much sir, I really enjoyed the day and my strange experiences too" Roger said with a grin on his face.

They headed to their cars. Kathleen told Pappy she would stay in touch and Roger said, "Follow me close Kath, traffic is bad at this time of day to my place, but I promise I won't lose you."

As Kathleen followed Roger, her thoughts returned to the day she had seen the ghosts. She wondered if Roger's sighting and hers had something to do with one another, and chills went down her arms. There were just too many darn coincidences, too many similar things that affected both her and Roger. They had only known one another for a very short time, but she was becoming convinced that their lives were headed in only one direction...she just wasn't sure where it was they were headed.

Chapter 19

It took 30 minutes to get to Roger's house. He was true to his word; he had stayed close and not lost her.

Kathleen followed Roger up to his side door. "Watch out, Kahlua will probably jump up on you; she loves visitors, especially pretty females. I've sent her to obedience school twice, but she still jumps on people."

Roger unlocked the door and Kahlua bounded up to the door, jumped up on Kathleen and licked her right in the face. "Ah, hi girl, I like you too" she said as she wiped the dog slobber off her face and petted the big dog.

"I need to take Kahlua for a short walk, there's wine on the kitchen counter. I think we'll both need a glass to fortify us before we start on the trunk. Glasses are in the cabinet just above the wine. The kitchen is to the right there." He pointed as he hurriedly clipped a leash on the dog and went out the door.

I headed in the direction Roger had pointed to, viewing the scenery as I went. The house was huge, just like the one next door where we had met. I figured this to be at least a $1 million dollar house, and felt a little intimidated. *It's a shame his parents had died recently, I don't think this is a house Roger would have picked for himself. He just didn't seem the type for a showplace like this.*

I found the kitchen, the wine and the glasses and poured us each a glass. I sipped on mine as I looked around the huge, ornate room. The walls were a cheery yellow and the floor was an expensive looking wood I couldn't identify. I could see the back yard through floor-to-ceiling windows that showed an Olympic sized pool. I heard Roger and Kahlua enter the door, and headed back to the counter to meet them. I handed Roger his wine and greeted Kahlua. She didn't jump up on me this time, guess she felt like I was OK to be in her house now.

Roger looked at Kathleen intently with a look that made her slightly uncomfortable and then he smiled and said "Follow me!"

Roger led the way up the winding staircase and made a right. We passed several bedrooms and two bathrooms and came to another small staircase. We went up and opened the door. Roger turned on the lights and I saw a massive attic.

It was not like the attic in my parent's house that only had one dim light bulb, lots of cobwebs, a lot of dust, no paint on the walls and thin slits of boards you had to walk carefully on or you would fall through to the room below.

This attic was painted pale beige, had carpeting on the floor and had fluorescent lighting in the ceiling. It was neatly packed with boxes and trunks. There was furniture that looked new, not old castaways like in some attics. Roger headed for a very large trunk that had a domed lid.

"I've only been up here a couple of times but I could tell from the description in Mom and Dad's will that this was the trunk of my ancestor. Dad was not interested in history to my knowledge, or maybe he just never got around to talking about it."

They walked over to the trunk and found an envelope addressed to Roger sitting on the top. They looked at one another and Roger said, "I wonder what this is, they didn't mention any letter and this was not here the last time I was up here?"

"I don't know, but you'd better open it. Would you rather I leave while you read it?" Kathleen asked.

"No, I think I might need you here for moral support while I do read it," he replied.

Roger carefully opened the envelope and took out two hand-written pages and began reading the letter out loud.

"My dear Roger, I leave you this trunk of your ancestor, William Barnes, who served in the 63rd Ohio Volunteer Infantry, Company C. He was a Corporal in that Company and served bravely until his death at Kennesaw Mountain. His unit was held in reserve there, but he was sent out as a scout and was mortally wounded.

I have never mentioned him to you, nor told you about this trunk for several reasons. First, there have been rumors passed down through several generations to me that the trunk may be haunted or hold some mystical secret. I have always been superstitious, and therefore never opened the trunk.

Second, the trunk moved by itself from one location in this attic to another when we first moved here, I know that sounds far-fetched, but I swear to you it happened. So, I have not been back up here. I am leaving this letter to let you make up your own mind about what to do about it.   I would have destroyed it but your Mother insisted that I not, she said there may be something there you were intended to see. I hope I am doing the right thing.

Your

loving father"

Chapter 20

Roger slowly folded the pages and put them back in the envelope. He was thinking to himself that the last week had been strange in his normal everyday life, and that things that had recently happened to him did not happen to most people in a lifetime. He was just thinking that a trunk could not possibly be haunted or mystical when the trunk lid flew open.

He jumped back from the trunk and Kathleen, who had been looking at the trunk and wondering what it could possibly hold, saw the lid open and immediately fainted onto the soft carpeting of the attic.

Roger ran to Kathleen's limp form and lifted her into his arms and began speaking to her "Kathleen, are you OK? Wake up please, please don't leave me with this thing all by myself."

She came around slowly, opened her eyes and looked into his and said, "Did I really see what I think I saw?"

"Yes" Roger said, "but please don't faint on me again. I don't want to be here by myself." He gently lifted her to her feet and they both stared at the trunk.

"I guess the trunk is telling us something. Are you willing to look inside with me?" Roger asked.

Kathleen took a deep breath, reached for his hand and said, "I guess I'm willing if you are, and if you promise to not leave me here alone."

They both peered into the trunk. The first item they saw was a quilt. Kathleen reached for it first and lifted it out. "Oh, it's lovely" she said. "I've seen this pattern before. It's called an Ohio Star. I think my grandmother made one like this. It looks like it was just made, but it must have been quilted over 100 years ago."

Roger reached in and picked up a shirt. "This looks really old too, looks like it was made by hand also...look at the odd stitches around the button holes. Don't think I've ever seen one quite like it."

Next was a dress, very plain and kind of ugly in today's standards, but I'm sure it was beautiful back when it was made. The fabric was beige and green, and it looked very fragile.

We carefully put aside the dress and shirt and quilt. Next was a pair of men's trousers, made of blue wool. We set those aside and saw a packet of letters.

Roger reached in and carefully pulled them out. They were yellow and brittle from age. "Let's take them over to the chairs and sit down and read them, there are a lot of them, so this may take awhile."

The first one he opened was addressed to William. The envelope read:

In care of the 63rd Regiment, Ohio Volunteer Infantry, Company 'C', for Corporal William Barnes. It was dated April 17, 1864.

"This must have been from William's wife" Roger said. "I'll read it out loud" he said.

My dear William, it has been so long since I have seen your face or touched your hand. I feel so bereft, I miss you so. I wrote this letter last week but have not heard from you in over a month and I don't even know where to send this. The last I heard from you was when you were headed for Resaca, Georgia. I pray you are safe, that you will return to me soon and that you and your unit have enough provisions.

I made you a shirt and pants and me a new dress this winter. Fabric is so scarce, but I was able to purchase some from Mrs. Wilkins, our neighbor. She lost her husband and two sons at Chickamauga and had no need for the fabric. Our town has lost so many; fathers, sons, brothers – will this war never end?

I made candles this week, used the berries that I saved from the Chinaberry tree in the yard. I also made soap and scented it from the bayberry plants from our neighbor's farm.

I hope I hear from you soon so that I can post this letter and send you the shirt and pants.

Your loving wife,

Catherine

"How awful to not even be able to send a letter to your loved one!" Kathleen exclaimed. "I guess it might have taken months to get a letter during the war. I never heard of a Chinaberry, have you?" she asked Roger.

"No, I haven't," Roger replied, "But here is a reminder that if you wanted candles or most anything else you could not go to Wal-Mart. You had to make it yourself or travel by wagon, horse, or on foot to the nearest general store. They lived in rural Ohio, so it's more likely they made most everything they needed. I was looking at this shirt; it's well made and sturdy, like the people of that time."

Kathleen looked at the next letter in the bundle. It was dated May 20, 1864, and the envelope was inscribed to 'Catherine Barnes, Chester, Ohio':

My Dearest Cath,

The battle at Resaca here in Georgia is over with heavy loss to the Union, and yur wish that this war will end is far from site, and I beleve it is the falt of the generals, specially our very own army general James McPherson. We was driving the rebs hard coming out of a gap in the hills at Resaca, could have taken the little village and get behind the rebs and cut them off. Me and the boys was on skirmich, we crossed a creek and cut their rail line, when we was ordred back by McPherson. He got the frites that he would be out numbered and decided to wait for the rest of the army. We got word that old Uncle Billy Sherman was madder than a wet hen. We had to attck the rebs and it was two days of hell, but I survived the attack on the hills in front of us which we took, but the rebs put up a fight at the los of many a man. Yes, my deerest, I too am so tired of this war and wish above all things to be back on our ground near Chester with yu and our little ones, but I rekon since we are fiten the rebs on their own ground, we need to press on and complet this thing.

I stll await the shirt I asked fore while summer is coming the weather is cool and wet and the shirt would be welcome as we has been on the march an have not been resupplied very much. My shoes is wering out, got hols in my britches and soks but recon the army will give me thes, but could still use the shirt.

> *I remain yur loving husband,*
> *William*

"I am so tired of this war," he wrote, Roger said, reflecting on his Civil War ancestor's words. "It's as if nearly 150 years have fallen away, and we can look into their minds like we were there with them, the soldier and his wife longing for the long bloody war to end, longing for peace, longing to be reunited."

Kathleen looked down at the letter and held it. "You know, by the time William wrote Catherine, the war had killed thousands of men. Antietam, Gettysburg and Chickamauga had soaked the soil with blood...had left thousands of widows and orphans and children who would grow up with only a memory of their fathers, North and South. And the bloodiest part of the fight for Atlanta was yet to come."

"That's true, that's so true Kath."

Kathleen smiled at the abbreviation of her name.

"You called me Kath, just like William called Cath in his letter."

"Sorry, don't know exactly why I did, I hope you don't mind."

"No, I don't, if you don't mind me calling you 'Rog'."

They both laughed; a relief from the seriousness that had come from reading the letters.

"Here is another letter to Catherine, but it is not from William," Roger said as he lifted the faded envelope, opened it and began reading.

July 5, 1864

Mrs. Barnes, it is my sad duty to inform you of the death of Corporal William Barnes, your husband, who was felled by enemy fire on June 27ᵗʰ during the recent fighting at Kennesaw Mountain. While our regiment was held in reserve, Corporal Barnes was part of a platoon detailed to support the assault on Little Kennesaw Mountain, and was struck by an enemy bullet while bravely leading other members of Company 'C', two of whom also died. I want you to know Corporal Barnes was a fine soldier and a credit to the company.

With deepest respect and praying you receive the care and comfort of our Lord at this time.

David Lasley
Captain, Commanding
Company 'C'
63rd Infantry Regiment

"I think your Mom was right, there is something in this trunk just meant for you to see, and now that we've met and seem to be connected to all this somehow, I think it was meant for me to see too."

"And he never got the shirt Catherine made for him did he?" Kathleen said, tears falling slowly down her face.

"No, it's been preserved in this trunk," Roger replied. "This time capsule that holds the belongings, the feelings and hopes in that tragic war...You know, reading this, I can feel the sadness, the longing, almost see the tears on her face when Catherine read this. So sad...so sad."

Chapter 21

Roger was leaning over my shoulder as I picked up the next item in the chest, a delicate golden locket on a thin golden chain. "This is really beautiful, looks like it probably predates the Civil War!" I said.

I opened the locket and gasped at what I saw. The woman looked like me and the man looked like Roger! Only a moment later Roger took hold of the locket and looked at me and said, "She looks like you and he looks like me, what in the world is going on here?"

In the instant Roger verbalized the words we were transported back in time, back to late June 1864, back to the time of the Battle of Kennesaw Mountain.

Roger and I looked at each other, looked around, but speech failed us both.

We stood outside a deserted log cabin on a red, muddy road...somewhere...we had no idea where, and rain was beginning to fall. As we looked around, the trees and foliage were filled out, as if it were late spring or early summer, and there was distant thunder, but it did not sound like an oncoming storm, there was more of a throaty rumble to it.

Roger looked at me for a long moment, his face expressing the same disbelief I know my face displayed.

"My God, Kath!" he exclaimed, "What's happened to us? Where are we? And why do you have on the dress that was in the trunk?"

"Gee Roger, I guess for the same reason you have on the shirt and pants that were in the trunk! Did I get hit on the head, because I am so confused, I feel like I have cotton in my brain! You're not playing some weird practical joke on me are you?"

"No, but I almost wish I were. I have a strange feeling we're not in Buckhead anymore, and it doesn't look like the year 2011 either. Do you suppose the locket in the trunk had something to do with this?"

We glanced up the road and saw a figure approach, an outline at first and then, drawing closer, the outline took the shape of a gawky teen with straw colored hair, wearing an ill fitting print shirt and patched cotton trousers that hung loosely from suspenders that looked like they were made of bed ticking. He also did not look like he came from our century. When he got close to us I said, "Excuse me young man, I seem to be a little confused today, could you tell me the date?"

He looked us over, probably thought I was as loony as I looked and replied, "Why of course ma'am, today is June 25th."

"And the year" I asked.

Then he really looked at me hard, like I was touched in the head, but he was polite. "It's 1864 ma'am, are you all right? Do I need to fetch someone to see about you?"

I shook my head and told him I was fine and thanked him for the information.

"Ma'am, don't mean to be telling you your business," he said abruptly as he was leaving us, "But if I was you, I would not stay in these parts long. The Yankees are coming. That's why this place is deserted.

That's why everybody else is gone. That's why I'm getting out of here right now! Best of luck to you both."

At that moment I realized the thunder I heard in the distance was not thunder. Suddenly there was an explosion in the sky, not 50 feet over our heads, frightening us both. Neither of us had seen the signs of war before. Now we were seeing it firsthand. I looked behind where we were standing and saw the mountain and knew it was Kennesaw.

Roger looked at me and I could tell he was totally bewildered when he said "Oh my God Kath, how could this have happened, and what do we do now? We've somehow gone back in time, back to the eve of the battle of Kennesaw Mountain. Remember we both touched the locket at the same time and said pretty much the same thing at the same time, that I looked like my ancestor and you looked like your ancestor. That has to be how we got here. Where's the locket now, do you have it?"

I felt around my neck, felt in both pockets of my dress, looked at Roger and shook my head. I knew instantly that meant there was no going back to my house or to my wonderful friends again. Tears fell slowly from my eyes as I remembered my life as it had been, but would never be again.

Roger wiped the tears from my face, kissed me tenderly and held both of my hands. "I'm afraid there will be no going back, is that what you were thinking to cause those tears?"

"Yes, that is exactly what I was thinking. Now we have to begin to live in another era, but at least we know our history and we know the area and what is about to happen. Do you realize that the battle is due to happen in only two days, we have to find shelter, food and more clothing before we do anything else."

Kathleen looked at the abandoned cabin by the road.

"Since there is no one here, this could be our shelter...and we may even find food and more clothing here," I said. We held hands and slowly walked into our new, but temporary home.

Chapter 22

The cabin was empty of food or clothing, but all the furniture and bedding was still there. I had read that people hid things before they left their homes, so I told Roger to look inside while I looked outside.

I walked to the back of the house and found a root cellar that had been hastily covered with dirt and straw. I brushed off the debris and opened the double doors. I carefully walked down the steep stairs and found sweet potatoes and what looked like jars and jars of pickles. At least we wouldn't starve for at least a couple of days I thought. I carried up some potatoes and a jar of pickles and headed to what looked like a smokehouse. It was dark and smelly inside. I walked around the entire insides and did not see a thing. As I was walking out I tripped over something on the floor. I bent down and saw a board sticking out. I leaned down and picked up the board and found beneath it several smoked hams. *Yoohoo!* I thought...*a feast for tonight if I can figure out how to start a fire and cook the hams and sweet potatoes.*

I walked back to the house and showed Roger the food I had found. He smiled at me and said he had found something too. He opened both his hands to show me gold coins. He had found them behind a loose brick in the fireplace.

"Well, now at least we have food and shelter and a little money, but you know we can't stay here more than tonight. We have to find the 63rd Ohio and find shelter that we know won't be in the line of battle."

"I've been thinking a lot while you were gone Kath, and I have to join up with the 63rd. I know it's risky, that I could be killed, but there is some reason we are here; something in that trunk made us go back in time to this battle. If my ancestor was brave enough to be here, then I've got to be brave enough to fight with him. Maybe there is some way I can help him or your ancestor, I just don't know, but I have to try."

"Oh Roger, I've just found you and I've fallen in love with you, I can't lose you now, please, please don't do this!" Tears rolled down my face and I ran to Roger and he held me in his arms.

"I've fallen in love with you too, and I wish with all my heart I could stay with you forever," Roger whispered to her. He put his finger under her chin and lifted her face and kissed her sweetly.

"I'm afraid my destiny has already been planned out for me. Somehow I was meant to be here...in this time and this place as were you. Let's make the most of it...maybe we can both make a difference somehow."

Chapter 23

Pappy Wilcox was wondering why he had not heard from his two new found young friends, his fellow historians whose lives had been affected by what they saw and felt at Kennesaw Mountain, so similar to what he once had felt and saw.

A full week had passed since Kathleen had promised to call and tell him what she and Roger found in that old trunk in the attic in Roger's home.

He had hesitated to call her, after all they really had just met and he did not want to seem pushy. Still, he was beginning to worry. They both had seemed so interested in the battle and the war and their ancestors.

When he read the front page of the morning paper, there was an answer that led to more questions, alarming questions.

"*Young Buckhead woman reported missing.*" The headline immediately caught his attention and as he read the story it alarmed him even more, for the young woman was identified as Kathleen Kelley, reported missing by her roommates and friends who told police this was not like her to disappear for several days and not let anyone know where she was. The story said foul play was suspected.

But then there was a companion piece, even more shocking to Pappy. It was a story about a missing young Atlanta engineer, Roger Barnes, who disappeared about the same time Kathleen Kelley had. Office friends and colleagues told police it also was not like him to suddenly vanish for several days and stay out of contact. No one drew a connection between the two missing young people, but Pappy did...he immediately did, and plainly saw that they had disappeared on the same day they went with him to the Mountain.

Now Pappy was really worried. What had happened? They had planned to go to Roger's house to look inside an old family trunk in the attic. Did something happen to them on the way to Roger's house? Did something happen at the house? Did it have to do somehow with the trunk? He was not only worried, he was afraid. Before he saw the ghost at Kennesaw Mountain he would have said he did not believe in the paranormal, but now he did. He knew there was the unexplained, and this was most certainly the unexplained.

He immediately went to the phone and dialed the number for the police. He was directed to a Detective Amy Simpson who answered on the second ring.

"Detective Simpson here" she said.

Pappy introduced himself and told her about his friends. "I know this sounds strange" he said, "I know we just met, but both of them had seemed so excited about finding out what was in the trunk in the attic, the trunk that held information about Roger's Civil War ancestor."

The detective listened carefully to what Pappy had to say. She hesitated a moment and then said "We did find something in the attic I would like you to take a look at. Could you come to the station today to meet with me?"

Pappy immediately agreed to meet her as soon as he could get there. He hung up the phone and cold chills ran down both his arms. He was afraid to go and see what they had found, but he was afraid not to go and not know what had happened. He said a silent prayer for his young friends, and quickly headed out the door.

Chapter 24

Amy Simpson, if anything, considered herself a practical, educated woman. Her profession demanded it, and that mindset had served her well as her reputation for solving cases that led to convictions indicated. There was always a reason for everything; logic, a pattern that would eventually reveal itself...it had simply been up to her to find it. She was sure there was a logical reason and a plausible explanation behind the disappearance of Roger Barnes and Kathleen Kelley.

He was young, wealthy, inheritor of the family fortune from his well-healed parents. Kathleen Kelley was also young, but not so wealthy, perhaps on the prowl for a rich husband. Her roommates had not described her that way. They were upset and distraught about why she was missing and suspected Barnes had something to do with that.

But Detective Simpson found nothing, so far, about Roger Barnes or Kathleen Kelley that indicated they would harm each other. There was no tragic or suspicious family backgrounds, except that Barnes' parents had both died in a car wreck; her parents, of natural causes. Neither one of them had any sort of record, except for a few minor traffic tickets. She could find no motive for anything criminal, and that is what she looked for first.

The first person she spoke to about Roger's disappearance was a well-known football player and next-door neighbor to Roger, Kevin Charles. He was also the first person to report Roger missing. He had been insistent that Roger would never have left his dog, Kahlua, alone in the house for any period of time without contacting his neighbor. It seems Kevin had a key to the house and often was contacted by Barnes to feed or walk the dog when he would be away for over a few hours. With Barnes gone, Kevin was caring for the dog.

She had Barnes' house completely and thoroughly searched from top to bottom. There was nothing to indicate any violence, but there was that thing, that little thing, that little locket, in plain view, sitting on top of that old trunk in the corner of the attic, as if someone had placed it there, hoping it would be found. That trunk would not budge, even when a muscular member of her search team tried to force open the lock. It just sat there, daring them. And now the old man, Professor Charles Wilcox, had told her they had gone to look into that trunk, trying to find out about his ancestor, for some reason, something about the Civil War, as she recalled. Wilcox was on his way to her office. She hoped he would have a clue, an answer...a logical answer to this because she was stumped, and Detective Simpson did not like to be stumped.

Pappy knew and had known law officers over the years, but had never met a lady detective so he did not quite know what to expect when he was escorted back to Detective Amy Simpson's office. He had imagined a tall, slender, dark-haired and dark-eyed assertive woman. She had sounded polite enough on the phone, but a little abrupt, a kind of down to business type person.

He found a perky, freckle-faced, smiling red head with bright blue eyes that welcomed him when he walked in, and her manner, no longer abrupt, was warm and inviting.

"Well, have a seat Professor Wilcox, take a load off and relax, I don't bite" the red headed officer said. "Your friends call you 'Pappy' don't they? Do you mind if I call you Pappy? Professor Wilcox sounds so formal."

Pappy looked at the investigator, deciding she was trying to get him to relax and did not suspect him of any wrong doing.

"No that's fine, don't mind at all."

Detective Simpson took the gold locket on its gold chain out of her front desk drawer and put it on her desk in front of Pappy.

"What do you know about this?" she asked, picking up the locket by its chain and handing it over to him.

"I know absolutely nothing about it. Where did it come from, where did you get it?" Pappy asked.

"It was sitting on top of the trunk in plain view, as if waiting for someone to see it, to pick it up," Simpson replied.

Pappy let his fingers examine it, feel its smooth, shiny yellow surface, simple but elegant, something common folk might be inspired to save all their hard earned wages to purchase, to be cherished, to be remembered.

"Well, it's quite old" he said, looking up at the detective. "I guess you already knew that, but as to how old, I'm not sure. I'm no expert on jewelry, but from what I've seen I'd say its mid-19th century at least. Have you tried to open it yet?"

"No," Simpson replied, hoping Pappy would offer to do that. "No I haven't. I don't know how."

"It's deceivingly simple, actually. Lockets were pendants or medallions opened to reveal two halves called wings" Pappy explained. "The ones I've seen were part of a soldier's personal effects that contained a picture of his wife, or sweetheart, or his children, and you have to take care opening the really old ones, like this one appears to be."

Pappy could see that this locket was large enough to hold small frames behind which quite possibly there were period photographs, 'images', people of that time called them. They were usually worn on a chain around the neck, but could also be part of a key chain or bracelet. This one appeared to be a neck chain.

Pappy knew it was very important that he took care to familiarize himself first with the proper technique for opening it. He did not want to damage it.

He placed the edge of his fingernail into the space between the two wings and moved his nail back and forth until the latch opened and the wings came apart.

Pappy was so pre-occupied with the locket he did not notice that Simpson was watching him carefully, following his every move. It was her nature to do so professionally as a close observer, but she was also curious about the old fellow and his fascination with this thing of antiquity.

Her office had become silent, she did not speak and he did not speak as he examined the locket. She broke the silence when it opened.

"Well!" she said, "I see you've been successful, you've opened a window on a piece of history here."

Pappy did not reply...he couldn't. He could not take his eyes off the images staring back at him from this tiny jewel piece. He wanted to speak, but could not. His throat was dry and choked, but Simpson saw immediately the cloud of disbelief, mixed with astonishment and sorrow that gripped his face.

"What is it Pappy? What?" Amy Simpson cried out. "What's wrong?"

The faces of Roger Barnes and Kathleen Kelley were looking back from time at him. Their expressions were solemn, but their eyes were fixed, often the look of people in photographs of long ago. They were dressed in clothing of the mid-19th century.

Pappy looked up at Simpson. "Where did you say you found this?"

"I told you, we found it sitting on top of the old trunk and the trunk was sitting in the corner," Simpson answered. "Pappy what did you just see? I know you saw something that upset you."

The detective reached over her desk, taking the locket away from him, and looked into it.

"There's nothing here, there's nothing in this locket," she said. "But you saw something, didn't you Pappy. What did you see?"

The professor, the living historian, who had seen and handled so many artifacts from the tragic war that split America in the mid 1800's knew immediately what had just happened.

The exposure of the photographs to the atmosphere had dissolved them, they had simply disappeared, just as Roger and Kathleen had disappeared, only now Pappy knew or had an idea how it happened.

That old trunk was possessed or enchanted, and somehow Roger and Kathleen's contact with the locket inside had taken them away and back in time. But it was too much for even him to take in right now and he knew the police detective would not understand, would not believe, so he would try to tell her something she could accept.

"Detective, I saw two images in the locket that resembled Roger Barnes and Kathleen Kelley and it was a shock at first...something unexplained, but we both know it is just an interesting coincidence, don't we? The images were preserved in the locket, but they were so old that when I opened the locket and air hit them they dissolved. I've seen it happen time and time again, and of course, it's a great loss, but I'm sure that's what happened."

"Curious...very curious," Simpson said, knowing she was now no closer to solving the disappearance of Roger Barnes and Kathleen Kelley than when she first started.

"Could I have that locket? That is when you're finished with it?" Pappy asked.

"Don't see why not, but for now we need to hold on to it as possible evidence. After all, it may be the last thing they had contact with."

"Yes, that's true," Pappy replied. "That is so true."

Chapter 25

The dawn of June 26, 1864 was unusually cool and windy and smelled of rain, with frowning skies overhead and not a patch of blue.

Roger and Kathleen had decided before they left the cabin they better have something to show their friendship and good will to the advancing Union troops, in particular Company C of the 63rd Ohio.

A farm wagon was parked in back of the cabin and in the pasture Roger could not believe his next find, a mule that the cabin owners for some reason had left behind.

He could not figure out why. The animal was not lame or diseased. Maybe they got out in such a hurry they loaded their belongings on another wagon to speed their departure and did not want to be delayed. That might also explain why there was so much food left in the cabin.

They loaded hams and sweet potatoes onto the wagon and headed up the road towards Sherman's advancing blue coats, just as the ominous sky made good its threat and began to pummel them with rain drops.

"I miss the automobile right now," Kathleen said, wiping her wet bangs from out of her eyes. "A little rain never hurt anyone" Roger said.

"Yeah, well, you're a guy and I'm a girl, and girls don't like to get wet and ruin their hairdo," said Kathleen as she wiped rain from her eyes again.

"How much further do you think till we meet up with the 63rd" Roger asked?

"It's hard to tell without all the tall trees from the 21st century, but I don't think it's much further." Just then they rounded a bend in the trail they were following and saw tents in the distance.

"That must be them" said Kathleen. When they got closer, two soldiers stepped from behind a tree, pointed their rifles at us and one ordered "Halt! That's far enough, what are you doing out here? State your business!"

Roger immediately spoke to the young private "Sorry sir, we just heard the 63rd Ohio was in these parts and we're bringing food for them, some nice hams and some sweet potatoes. You see, we're Union sympathizers living here in Georgia for the past two years, we came here from Ohio and we wanted to see if I could join up with this regiment?"

"You'll have to talk with my Corporal. Gustov, go get Corporal Kelley."

The private took off on the double quick. In just a moment a bantam rooster of a soldier approached them, clearly irritated.

"Wilson, you've pulled guard duty long enough to know you're supposed to call out 'Corporal of the Guard!', and not send somebody after me, and besides you've let these civilian strangers too close to the camp anyway. I ought to put you on report for this!"

"But Corporal," Wilson said, gulping and sweating and clearly dreading his name on report, "They're friendlies...they're Ohio folks like us, been hidin' out in Reb country and they brought food!"

"You know all that by taking their word...is that right?" Corporal Kelley replied, getting more red faced. "You never laid eyes on them before in your life and don't know if that food is poisoned or not!"

Kathleen was watching Corporal Kelley closely. He had the male Kelley traits so familiar to her, in her father, her uncle, and her cousins. Short but muscular...bantam roosters all of them, with short tempers, but all mild as pussy cats underneath that rough bravado.

"Corporal Kelley, I do apologize for disrupting your camp. We truly only came to give you some of our food, some ham and sweet potatoes, and to see if Roger here could join up with you." She batted her pretty green eyes at the Corporal and said "By the way, my name is Kathleen Kelley, of the Columbus, Ohio Kelley's, could we possibly be related?"

The Corporal immediately changed his tune, doffed his cap, and said smilingly "I do apologize Miss Kelley, but we don't often encounter civilians and we have to be careful, there are spies about everywhere I'm told. I don't know of any Kelley's from Columbus, but you sure do look like a Kelley, that's for certain."

"Did you say hams? Why I sure do fancy ham."

He thought over the situation for just a moment and said "Come on in camp and sit down and tell me more about yourselves."

"Private Wilson, go back to your guard duty. I'll escort these two to camp personally." The Private thought his Corporal had changed his tune awful fast like, but he did as he was told.

Corporal Benjamin Kelley displayed another family trait when he removed his dusty dark blue forage cap to wipe his head and face with his handkerchief; the fiery red hair of the Kelley clan. Kathleen saw right away it was the same as her father's and all the male members of the family she knew of, only now she saw where they got it from.

"You all sit down and take a load off" he said as they arrived at the camp fire site, and invited them to take a seat in some folding camp chairs placed around the fire pit.

The red headed corporal decided the man and woman were safe, and probably who they said they were and what they said they were. After all, she was in no hurry just to give them the hams and potatoes, and he was asking to join the company and fight the Rebs.

But he was still curious.

"How is it you two came down here two years ago with the war in progress and no Northerners likely to be welcome in these parts?" he asked.

"I came to work on the railroad" Roger replied, and Kathleen immediately realized he was preparing their cover story.

"I'm an engineer, I design and build railroads, and at the time I came to see about my aunt and uncle in Marietta near here and Kathleen came with me. But I never saw eye to eye with the Rebel cause and wished many times I could have stayed up north and enlisted.

Until my relatives passed on, Kathleen and I just made the best of it until you fellows arrived, then we saw our chance."

Corporal Kelley looked at the young woman. There was something familiar about her, she somehow had family traits he recognized, the red hair, the fair skin, the green eyes, with the stature of the Kelley women. How could that be, he wondered. She said she was from Columbus, but none of his Kelley's hailed from there.

Corporal Kelley looked at her young companion.

"You said you would have enlisted if you had stayed up north, by the way, where do you hail from in Ohio and what is your name?" he asked.

"I am Roger Barnes from near Akron, by way of Meigs County, down on the Ohio River," Roger replied. "Ma and Pa came up from Chester."

Kelley rubbed his grizzled chin, glancing over at a stack of muskets whose owners had no more use for them. Battles and skirmishes had taken its toll on Company C since they first met the Rebels in the fighting at Resaca.

"Well, Barnes, you just might get your chance to fight for Ohio and the Union yet. We've had a number of dead and wounded and could use a man who wants to fight, only thing is, do you know how to fight? Have you seen the elephant?"

"I drilled with the militia before I left Ohio," Roger replied. Since Kathleen had awakened his interest in the war he had read everything he could find, especially about the life of the common soldier and how he was taught to drill and fight. He felt he was on the verge of meeting, like Kathleen had, the man in Company C he was descended from, William Barnes.

Chapter 26

I wonder if this has ever happened to anyone else on earth, at anytime or any where. Roger reflected as he looked around the Company C camp, at this place in time, at these people that existed over a hundred years before I was born.

Roger and Kathleen were alone for a moment back at the farm wagon they had driven into the camp with its welcome load of food. Corporal Kelley was about the business of rounding up a uniform for Roger, along with equipment and a musket so he could be assigned to a platoon that very likely would be on the skirmish line the next morning. There was word that a big battle was coming, a big push to break the rebel line and if successful it would be the campaign right here at the mountain.

"I've read fictional stories about time travel" Kathleen replied. "I don't know, but I don't think anyone has actually done it. It is still so unbelievable, so incredible I can't believe this has happened. I'll never see anyone I know and love again. My God Roger, it's almost as if we are already dead."

They turned to see a young Corporal approaching them. His hands were full of clothing and a black slouch hat. He had on a dusty uniform that looked like it had seen its share of hard marching and campaigning. Roger was struck immediately by the man's face. It was as if he was looking at his father who had come back to life.

"Hi ya, I'm William Barnes and you must be Roger Barnes. Can't rightly figure it but you look familiar somehow. I guess we're both Barnes so maybe that's why. You reckon we're related somehow? Anyway, don't know if this sack coat and trousers will fit, but the fella they used to belong to was close to your size and maybe the hat will fit too."

Roger was looking at Corporal Barnes and knowing his ancestor's fate he was again reminded of the incredible, unbelievable circumstance he was in. Roger thought if it was at all possible to change fate, he would save his ancestor from dying tomorrow, but he had a feeling in his gut that fate could not be changed.

"Thanks Corporal, I'll try them on but they look like they'll fit just fine."

"Well that's good, after you try them on why don't you and your lady come to the fire and have a piece of that ham and those sweet potatoes you were kind enough to bring us. Maybe by then Kelley will have a rifle and some equipment for you to use. Looks like you're going to need it by tomorrow morning. We heard there's going to be a big fight shortly after first light."

Roger, Kathleen and Corporal Barnes were finishing supper when Kelley approached them carrying a musket and equipment.

"Found this Springfield in pretty good shape, and here's a belt, cap box, canteen and cartridge box for ya. Could not find a spare haversack but maybe we'll get one in the morning and we'll draw your ammunition then. You and Corporal Barnes will be in the platoon that's part of the skirmish line while the rest of Company C will be held in reserve. I guess your lady will be staying the night. I'll get her a couple of blankets and she can sleep under your wagon. You can sleep with the rest of us. I have to go see about the guards for the night, I'll see you tomorrow."

Kathleen sat at the campfire, sipping on a cup of lukewarm coffee. She had tuned out Roger and Corporal Kelley's conversation and was thinking of what would happen tomorrow. If Roger died in the battle, what would she do? Where would she go and how could she provide for herself? She was not familiar with 1860's Georgia. She had read a lot about the area, but reading and being there were two completely different things.

She couldn't help but think how ironic life was; she had found the love of her life at last and she may lose that love tomorrow. She hoped with all her heart that Roger would survive, but she had to prepare for the possibility that he might not.

She heard the conversation ending and looked up at Roger with a heavy heart. She must put on a brave face for him...she couldn't let him see the sadness that pervaded her very soul.

"Corporal Kelley suggested you sleep under the wagon, he's gone to have someone get you some blankets" Roger said. "He intends for me to sleep with the rest of the Company. Let's walk over to the wagon while we're waiting on those blankets."

They walked slowly, hand in hand, both lost in thoughts of tomorrow. "I'll miss being with you tonight, but I'll see you in the morning" Kathleen said as she reached up and kissed his cheek.

"I've been thinking Kath, if anything happens to me tomorrow I promise I will never really leave you. Remember those ghosts we saw. If they can do it, come back in time that is, then I can too. I'll come back to you. I promise I'll be with you forever." They held hands, remaining silent, but joined together in their hearts, not thinking about what would happen tomorrow but only of this moment, of being together.

Chapter 27

The awakening of men at war about to deliver death and have death delivered upon them roused Kathleen from a fitful sleep in her refuge beneath the farm wagon. The beginning of June 27, 1864, was making itself known with the sun's first rays from the eastern horizon. At first there was a grayish light in which the soldiers in dark and light blue moved about, appearing like phantoms. Then the light increased to more clearly reveal their features.

Kathleen had hardly needed Corporal Kelley's blankets for warmth; the night was humid and she had placed them between herself and the bare moist earth.

Members of Company C huddled around their campfire cooking coffee. The smoke rising into the beginning of a blue sky that would soon burn away the moisture of this unusually wet, autumn-like June and bring a pitiless brightness and heat.

Roger, now dressed in his blue coat and sky-blue trousers, wore his black hat with the brass letter "C" jauntily tilted on his head. He was one of the soldiers at the fire, waiting for the coffee to boil.

He glanced over at the wagon and saw Kathleen awake and rising. Just then the coffee boiled and William Barnes reached over and carefully removed the pot from the fire with his handkerchief. Roger borrowed a spare cup from one of the soldiers and poured a cup for Kathleen. He brought it to her and smiling at her said "Good morning, how did you sleep under this wagon? Be careful, this cup is hot."

Kathleen looked up at him smiling and gingerly accepted the hot coffee from him. "Well obviously I couldn't undress in a camp full of men, so I slept in my clothes and did not sleep well. Did you get any sleep" she asked?

"Kelley found a blanket for me and I wound up sleeping by the fire. I guess I slept most of the night, I was pretty tired."

They both fell silent, as Kathleen sipped on her hot, strong coffee. Roger was the first to break the silence, as he leaned over and whispered in her ear "We don't have much time left you know, where will you go during the battle? Please stay safe my love, and I'll try to do the same."

Kathleen hesitated a moment, then said "I guess I'll stay here at the wagon and pray for your safe return."

William Barnes approached them from the campfire. "They're calling for us to form up for the skirmish line, it looks like things are about to start."

Roger turned to Kathleen, "Goodbye love, I'm sure Corporal Kelley will watch over you." He kissed her tenderly and the two soldiers walked away.

Roger's platoon detached from Company C was already moving toward the underbrush when the Federal artillery started. The thump, thump, thump of the cannons was unnerving to Roger, unaccustomed to the sound of battle. The line halted in a dense thicket; a blend of tall pine and hardwood trees was overhead. William Barnes reached into his coat, retrieving his pocket watch. "Eight o'clock!" he said, grinning slightly and glancing over at Roger. "Looks like old Billy Sherman wants to wake the Rebs up and get things started early."

The skirmishers, a few yards ahead of them, fired their rifles, signaling Roger and William's line to move forward. They approached a narrow, muddy creek. Beyond it they could see Rebels loading and firing at them. Roger had read about the zipping sound mine' balls made, but now he saw and heard it firsthand. One round clipped a pine tree next to him, knocking off a piece of bark that struck his shoulder. "Get low!" William cried out. "Them Rebs have us in their sights!" William and Roger fired and the skirmishers in their rear advanced past them and forded the muddy, dirty creek. "Next time, it will be our turn to get wet and dirty" William said as he reloaded. "That creek don't look too wide, but we'd better get across and out of it in a hurry."

The skirmishers ahead fired again. Roger, William and the others hit the muddy water, hurriedly struggling to get across. Just as they emerged into the woods on the other side, Roger heard the thud of lead striking flesh, and beside him William crumpled and fell to the ground, dropping his rifle and gripping his midsection with his hands. He looked at Roger, "God! Gut shot! I am gut shot!" he yelled as he rolled to his side. Roger saw the blood gushing from this soldier who was his ancestor, who in less than a day and night had become his friend.

William had told him of his life at home, how much he loved his wife Catherine, and longed to return and resume his life with her. Roger, of course, could not tell the truth about himself. How could William understand or believe him. How could Roger understand and believe what was happening, yet it was. His family history played out in front of him.

"You better get up and move on!" William gasped, "Ain't nothin' you can do for me."

"No, William, let me get you back to a surgeon."

William coughed up blood, laughed and then grimaced. "Hell, I'd rather die here peacefully under the trees than have them damn butchers back there kill me quicker by carving on me. This is a gut wound, ain't nothin' they can do with me no how."

Roger looked up to see the Rebels aiming their rifles once more. He saw the puff of smoke, and heard the crackling sound of their volley. Then he heard and saw nothing else. An Enfield round smashed into his head, between his eyes. Roger Barnes, from the year 2011, fell dead beside the man he had come to know and like, Corporal William Barnes, his Civil War ancestor, from 1864.

Chapter 28

Kathleen sat against a small scrawny pine tree and listened to the gunshots in the distance. Her mind drifted to her friends and her home, to things she knew she would never see again, then back to Roger and his ancestor William and the terrible battle she knew was taking place. Her stomach growled and she longed for a cheeseburger and french fries. She got up and headed to the abandoned campfire, hoping to find something to eat. All she found was a bucket of water which she drank from, hoping to quiet her rumbling stomach.

She saw off in the distance four men, heading slowly toward her and she knew instantly that Roger had been killed. Sadness flowed over her in great waves, almost like the sadness that had engulfed her that first day she visited Kennesaw Mountain. Rivulets of tears rolled down her cheeks, and she sobbed openly.

The first to approach was Corporal Kelley. He walked up to her and put his large hands on her shoulders "I'm so sorry Kathleen, but Roger and William were both killed just over that ridge there, they died next to one another. It was quick, Roger didn't suffer. We buried 'em both, next to the creek. He was a brave lad, he didn't have to join in and fight like he did."

Tears trickled down his face and he abruptly turned and walked away. The other three men walked up and offered their condolences.

One Private introduced himself as Charlie, and told her he had heard of a plantation less than half a mile to the south that had been abandoned and that the owners had moved permanently farther to the South and were not planning on returning.

"You could stay there a spell, don't think anybody would bother you," Charlie said.

The day was so hot, must have been 100 degrees. She laid on the ground and cried herself to sleep for a short time, awakening to more gunfire in the distance.

I can't stay here...I've got to get away, everything and everyone I see reminds me of this horrible day she said out loud to herself. My God! My God! Roger...why did this have to happen to us.

She found the mule grazing near the wagon, hitched it and left for the place Charlie had spoken of.

He was right. The sign on the fence surrounding the small plantation read *"Fuller's Plantation."* She opened the front door and walked into a small parlor. Most of the furniture was still there. She walked through the other rooms, those too almost completely furnished. Then she went up the stairs and found five large bedrooms, all had a bed and dresser but little else. Kathleen went to the first bed she found, lay down and cried herself to sleep again. Roger appeared to her in a dream.

He was in his uniform, holding his black hat. He whispered "I'll be with you soon, my love." She awoke looking for him, but he was not there.

She got up from the lonely bed where she had seen visions of Roger...or at least thought she had. She knew she had to try to get over this mind-draining sadness. She slowly walked down the stairs and looked around. The place was extremely clean for being uninhabited, she thought. I wonder why they would clean the place and then leave?

She was startled by a shadow in the kitchen and she screamed out.

"Shush, shush now miss, ya'll wake the dead!" A large black woman wearing an almost head-to-toe apron said to her. "Who're ya and whatcha doin' here?" she asked.

Kathleen was taken aback and stuttered "I'm Kathleen Kelley and I just lost the man I loved in the fighting over at the mountain. I'm lost and frightened, and..." Her voice broke and trailed into tears, tears and grief she could not stop.

"Here now, here little miss, you stop that cryin'. I'll make ya a nice cup of tea. That'll make ya feel better."

Kathleen sniffled and dried her tears on the arm of her dress. "Thank you, I would like that very much. What is your name?"

"Everyone calls me by the name of Mamma, but my god-given name is Bessie."

Bessie brought the tea to the table "Sorry, but we ain't got no sugar, not with that blockade and all, but the tea's good, now drink up."

Kathleen sipped the tea, it was very good. "So, why are you here? She asked. "I heard from a soldier over at the Mountain that no one lived here anymore."

"We stayed on here after Mr. and Mrs. Fuller moved on...to take care of the place. We know we free now, but we got nowhere else to go. We got a place about a mile back from here. My husband is named Jonathan, and we got five children." Bessie explained slowly to her. "You wouldn't make us leave would ya?"

"No, no of course not, I could really use your help if you don't mind." Kathleen said. She was thinking that these people could help her while she thought about what to do next. Maybe she could start a school for the newly freed slaves and their children; it could be a beneficial relationship for all concerned she decided.

Bessie looked at Kathleen and said "You're more than welcome to stay here; Lord only knows they's plenty of room, and plenty to do here to keep the place up."

Kathleen settled into a routine, helping Bessie with the house and the garden. She worked with Jonathan on building a schoolhouse and began to look forward to teaching. Each day she hoped to see Roger, and each day she did not. The days turned into weeks, and the weeks into months. Roger had promised her he would return and she knew he would if he could.

Exactly three months to the day of the Battle of Kennesaw Mountain, Kathleen awoke to someone whispering in her ear. She opened her eyes and there he was, at first she could barely make out a ghostly shape and then he was there in full form.

"I promised you I would never leave you Kath. It took me a while to figure it out, but I'm here now and I will be with you forever."

About the Authors

Lois Helmers is a native of Columbus, Ohio. She moved to Atlanta, Georgia in 1980 and is a graduate of Oglethorpe University. She published her first book, a non-fiction history and genealogy research book titled ***"Meigs County Ohio and Her Soldiers in the Civil War"*** in 2009. She is an amateur Genealogist, Historian and Civil War re-enactor. She is also an excellent quilter.

Gerald Harding Gunn or Jerry as he prefers to be called, has a lifelong interest in America's greatest and most tragic struggle, the Civil War. He has directed this interest toward stories influenced by that struggle. Jerry is a career broadcast and website journalist who developed a love for the Civil War era when he was a young boy. He has participated in living histories and reenactments, on and off, since the age of 15.

Jerry blends the past with the present in his first novel, *"A Rose for William Carter"*, and again with Lois Helmers in *"The Ghosts of Kennesaw Mountain"*. Jerry is a native Georgian, born and raised in Atlanta. He grew up there, surrounded by reminders of the Civil War in this city of *"Gone with the Wind."*

We hope you enjoyed this book. For more great stories by these authors and others, please visit our website at:

WWW.BadgleyPublishingCompany.com
Thank you and have a great day.